Dear Nicol(
Power of the

Love,
Andrew Steed

POWERING UP
OUR LIFE STORIES

Written by
Andrew Steed

Illustrated by Julia Jeffrey

**Grosvenor House
Publishing Limited**

This book is published by
Grosvenor House Publishing Ltd
28-30 High Street, Guildford, Surrey, GU1 3EL.
www.grosvenorhousepublishing.co.uk

A CIP record for this book
is available from the British Library

ISBN 978-1-78148-873-7

This Book is dedicated to my Mother & Father and the ancestors of my lineage. To Elizabeth Grace Davie and Anthony John Robert Steed thank you on your loving guidance and your support throughout the years. In gratitude to the ancestral clans the Innes & Davidson of the Matriarchal line and the Steed and Daines of the Patriarchal line may our song lines shine brightly and our stories bring laughter and learning for those who dance in our footsteps.

Dear Reader, Teacher, Student and fellow Authors of countless stories that are lived each day,

Welcome to the world of reclaiming stories.

This book is a result of years of working on reclaiming my own stories and helping countless others to reclaim theirs.

At the end of each chapter you will find a list of journal questions and journey questions. These are there to prompt the reader to peel away the layers of their own story. This is a book that requires us to walk into the depth of our own shadows to shine our light there, to transform our faeces into fertilizer.

For teachers/professors working with students this book is for you too. All of us need to do our own work so we can help others to do theirs.

My suggestion is that you read the first couple of chapters in order to give you a clear understanding of reclaiming. Then you can go to the chapters that call you.

Some of the questions will be easier to answer than others. Some you will be eager to dive in to. Others you may look to avoid. Notice where and when your resistance comes up. Do not try to answer the questions from each chapter all in one go. Be thorough, take your time and be willing to peel away the layers so you can journey to the core, the very centre of your own story. You will notice the bonus question. This book is written to help promote creativity, critical thinking and problem solving, attributes that are truly needed in our world.

There are some questions that are very light hearted and others that require great courage to step into. The journey is one of celebration. The most important piece is to not get stuck in the story. Reclaiming encourages us to shift, release and transform.

Some of your journaling will be for your eyes-only; other writings will be for sharing. You need to work out which is which. If a question seems too daunting or a journey overwhelming make sure you are working with a trusted teacher, counselor, or in the case of journeying, a shamanic practitioner who will support your process.

The shamanic element is there for those who have been called to journey in non-ordinary reality. For those who do not have an understanding of this an would like to know more you are welcome to email me at asteed@andrewsteed.com and I will look to link you with someone who can help you in your area. For those who have no interest in the journeying aspect please read through the journey questions. You may find that you can reframe them into journal questions for yourself to consider.

I have written the book choosing to use the spelling and language of my native land. If there are words or sayings that you do not immediately understand enjoy looking them up. Language is so delicious!

When I lived in the USA I visited a Laundromat, which in the British Isles is known as a Laundrette. I was busily emptying a washing machine when a woman who was in there struck up a conversation with me. We spoke for a few minutes and she asked where I was from. I told her the British Isles and she asked how long I had been in the States. My answer was 3 months to which she replied, "That's amazing." Baffled I asked her what was amazing. She looked me straight in the eye and said "Well you've picked up the language real quickly." She thought we all spoke German in Britain! Although this story has always tickled me there is an underlying truth. So many words used in England are foreign to Scotland and vice versa let alone taking into account the rest of the Isles, Canada, the USA and Australia, for that matter language differs wherever so called 'English' is spoken.

My hope is that this book will encourage us all to fly with more freedom, to soar higher and deepen our roots. Thank you for opening up the front cover; now enjoy delving into the treasures that wait within!

In love, truth, beauty and freedom,
Andrew Steed.

Acknowledgements

I am grateful on the flow of ideas that came through me to create this book. Thank you Joyce for being a major part of all aspects of this work. I love you. Your support, love, ideas, the endless cups of tea and reminding me to stop and eat as I journeyed into the chapters is beyond these words of gratitude. Thank you Julia Jeffrey and the fae who brought us together in Baltimore though we both were living in Glasgow. They knew we would bring our gifts together and shine more light into the world. Thank you Pam Cosgrove for the hours of editing. Your diligent approach has kept the energy of the book moving onwards and upwards.

Thank you Tom Cowan, Sandra Ingerman, Terri Smith, Adrian Adams, and Agnes M Toews for your words of encouragement and willingness to help this book reach the hearts and homes of people around the globe. Thank you Mary Carbaugh for your thoughts on bringing the stories to our youth. Thank you Gayle Cluck for opening the doorways into schools so that I have been able to work with countless teens on reclaiming their stories. Thanks to the many schools and colleges that have opened their doors to me, especially Central York School District and Elizabethtown School District in PA, USA. Sue Petersen, Nancy Warble, Lisa Sands, Ben Hodge, Cindy Hogentogler, Tara Goodrich, all of the professors, teachers, parents and students whose paths I have met working these ways in the last 15 years.

A huge thank you to my own two children Christy Robert Steed and Aylish Rose Colbert Steed who inspire me to be the best storyteller that a Dad can be. Thank you to Mark Gooden and all of my friends who came on adventures when we were teens. Thanks to Janette Hunt nee Lloyd who is my longest friend on the planet outside of family in this lifetime, just knowing that you are there and we can pick up wherever we left off brings ripples of laughter to my heart. Thanks to Mulina and Emerson Ludvigsen for your generosity of spirit, opening the doorway of friendship is a special treat and a treasured gift; you provide a wonderful sanctuary for me to integrate the work. Thanks to Janis Wemyss, Major Forbes and all at Corse House who provided the space for most of the writing to take place nestled by the fire in the old manor house. Thanks to all the unseen beings for your support and to the ancestors who love a great tale. Finally a massive thank you to Mrs. Howard, my first teacher at the Guildhall Feoffment primary school who brought stories alive inside of me and encouraged me to always believe in the magic.

Contents

Chapter 1

A Noble White Horse

"Make the mistakes of yesterday your lessons for today."
-Anonymous.

I love the smell of books. I love to touch them, flick through the pages and feel the paper between my fingertips, to check out the front cover and let my imagination tumble into thoughts of what adventures lie ahead. A great story feeds us on the breath of every word. Those of us fortunate enough to have sat in the presence of a master storyteller know the magic, we feel the wonder and we crave a little bit more. We hang on the sound of lilting tones, gasp during suspenseful pauses and eat up every word the silver-tongued wordsmith weaves in the telling. In short, stories provide a banquet for our senses. They stretch us, teach us and challenge us. We are connected through stories. Ancestral threads reminding us to remember the song of the past, the dance of the present and the poetry awaiting to meet us in the future. We are the characters in each and every tale; we are comprised of the light and the dark, the hero, the villain, the victim, the witness and the passerby. In between the spaces, beneath the surface, in a single word lie transformation, insight, and strands of magic waiting for a diligent seeker to unearth a casket of treasure. So often we skip ahead, gloss over the details and more often than not relegate stories and storytellers to child's play and no more. The truth is stories were never for the children and always for the children. They were danced, sung, weaved on the wind by the light of the fire since the beginning of time. They are a road map, a compass and a creative magical way for us to discover who we are and why we are here.

We are also the sum of the stories that we have lived and breathed during our time here on planet earth/planet water. All of our experiences stored in our personal filing cabinet the human body. Our ancestors were fully aware that singing, dancing and drumming helped us to remove energetic blocks that fester inside of us robbing us of valuable life force. The shamans, the bards, the medicine elders understood the importance of our stories being told, that some need reweaving and reclaiming to release the shards that would cut us energetically, leaving weeping wounds that bleed us dry. As I have worked with stories over the years I started to instinctively work with what is an ancient practice, the art of reclaiming our stories.

Stories intrinsically are powerful. Harnessing the power that is inherent in these stories takes the willingness to walk into our shadows to shine our light there. I discovered that rewriting a disturbance in my past creates a new vibrant reality as does illuminating a tale in its original format to glean the lessons of reclaiming in another way. Playing within the stories albeit tales of horror, adventure, embarrassment, failure and success has been a liberating experience. Each of us has chapters of wonder, heartache, challenge, despair, fun, fear and excitement to name but a few. These scenarios from our past are wrapped into our psyche locked in our minds and our bodies. To be able to delve into these, and change the outcome of the story, generates a healing vibration that frees us from the bonds that enslave us. This time honored tradition of our ancestors is rewarding and accessible to us all. I have worked a number of tales in this book showing different ways of reclaiming. There are treasures for each of us within these tales, my hope is that you will be moved to write, reweave and reclaim some of your own. The Celts were Master Storytellers who spun myths that still affect us today. Shamans all across the world were amongst the first storytellers. They knew the best way to teach was, and still is, by the story.

AN AFRICAN TALE OR THE TALE OF A BOX

A Western man traveled into the depths of the African jungle to visit a tribe who had recently received the gift of electricity but had never witnessed a television set. It was with great glee and anticipation that the man presented the tribe with his gift of a brand new state of the art colour TV. For the first couple of days everyone gathered to watch the intriguing new device. He was thrilled that his gift had made such an impression. Then as the week wore on less and less people appeared to watch it with him. By the end of the week the television was abandoned completely. This mystified the man so he sought out the leader and asked,

"Why are the people no longer watching the TV?"

"We have the storyteller," the chief stoically replied.

"Yes, but your storyteller will never know as many stories as the television does," spat back the Westerner.

"Your words speak true," agreed the Chief. "Your television may know more stories, but our storyteller knows us".

I remember as a kid seeing a colour television for the first time. The images beaming into my friends' house captivated me. There was prestige in owning such a device. Soon they were the mainstay in every home. They continue to get bigger and now it is uncommon to find a household without one or even with just one. I remember when we used to have to get up and change the channel and we only had three channels to watch. Now I look bamboozled at three remotes that control 100's of channels with more features than I care to understand. Television is one of the great sedatives of our time. We can fall into the habit of watching other people's stories at the expense of living our own.

Indigenous people have kept the stories alive, they left a blueprint within them. They knew and felt the innate value in the oral tradition of sharing our heritage. In the British Isles and Ireland we had Bards who were the keepers of the stories and songs. Here, in what we know as the Celtic lands, these ancestors would readily agree that it is essential to explore the old tales and our own stories to appreciate mythic patterns that flow through our own lives. Understanding our own story, allows us to grow, to move forward, to embrace and to live. This is a direct gift from our ancestors.

I have chosen several of my own life stories that I have reclaimed in different formats. These tales offer the reader a possible route to journey and journal on. I encourage you all to allow your creative sides to flourish. The questions at the end of each chapter are a guide to open a doorway for an intrepid traveler to walk through. Hopefully each of you will discover many treasures within yourselves by having the courage to take these steps. For here lies the opportunity for healing, change and self-growth. Beyond this my hope is that you will be inspired to begin reclaiming your own stories.

At the end of each story I have provided two lists. The first list is designed for people from all walks of life to journal on for self-discovery. The second list is for people who practice shamanism and know how to journey into non-ordinary reality. For those who are unfamiliar with this practice I suggest you read this book fully first and then if called seek out a reputable shamanic practitioner to guide you in this tradition. If exploring a shamanic pathway in this fashion does not sing in your heart then have fun playing with the journey questions to transform them into journal questions. What I know for sure is that stories are inherently shamanic.

So without further ado let's delve into the reweaving of a tale, spinning threads of the mythic heroic quest. Through reclaiming our story we empower ourselves by letting go of our past and rewriting our present.

A PAIN IN THE NECK

The original, disconcerting story, was one that I wanted to forget. It wasn't a deep scarring tale, however it was embarrassing to say the least. The punch line was such that was best described as being a pain in the neck.

I was a wild and reckless teenager. I loved to hitchhike, catch a bus, a train, jump in a car or even on occasions take a cab ride and head off to see live bands play. A list as long as my arm had enticed me across the length and breadth of the country. By 18 I had tasted the delights of The Jam, The Clash, The Police to name but a few- I even went to see Slade, though the icing on the cake was Bob Marley and the Wailers; I loved gigging. The only music that did nothing for me was heavy metal. AC/DC, Motorhead and the like were just not my cup of tea.

On a warm summers evening in 1981 I had hopped on the train from my hometown of Bury St. Edmunds in the heart of Suffolk to head to Ipswich. Goodness knows why, for I was off see a heavy metal band called Saxon at the Gaumont Theatre. I had friends who raved about the crash and grind of this ear-shattering screech that they called music and I called noise. One of my best friends Rob Waters was hooked on air guitar and the leather and denim-clad look of the many longhaired dudes who followed this racket. So I had tagged along with my mate Rob and a few other 'biker' friends, as I figured I had nothing better to do.

We often headed to Ipswich. The Gaumont was a regular haunt as was Portman Road the home of Ipswich Town F.C. I like my footie and although I have been a Chelsea fan since the age of 7 the 'Town' are the closest team to Bury St. Edmunds so I was often singing my heart out on the terraces in my youth. The football team have picked up the tag of 'Tractor Boys' today, however at their inception in 1878 they were more likely to have been the 'Ploughmen'. Their original crest was a red rampant lion, which was then replaced by the Suffolk Punch, a noble white horse. So we were headed to the town of the white horse not to jeer and cheer at a kicked ball of leather. Tonight the screams would be coming from a group of longhaired rockers from Barnsley and we would be gyrating our bodies to their screeching din.

One thing that you need to know about me is that I don't do things half-heartedly. So when the first metallic crash emanated from the guitar strings I rushed to the stage with the throng of people clambering to be at the front. We all took our imaginary guitars in hand. For the next hour and a half I played that invisible guitar like there was no tomorrow. It was a performance to remember; well I sure remembered it. As part of the guitar mimicking tradition, one swings the arm, plucks unseen strings and violently bashes the head up and down, known in technical terms as head banging. I have a very long neck on my tall slender frame, and that night I shook my head like an unbroken stallion trying to be bridled for the first time.

Once the smoke machines were switched off, and the band had worked their encore and played no more, we all piled out of the theatre. I grabbed a souvenir t-shirt for a couple of quid before I headed home. It was nice to take off my sweaty shirt and put on a clean one even if it did have 5 headshot portraits of the band with their name 'Saxon' emblazoned upon it.

I was shattered, I'd given it my all, my ears ringing with deafness, my body weary, and my mind ready to take this night into the world of dreams.

When the sun streamed through my window and the radio alarm blasted out the arrival of a new working day, I groggily tried to rise. My legs reached for the floor, my torso pushed forward in a lazy attempt to greet the morning, and that's as far as I got. My head was anchored firmly to the bed, and no matter how hard I tried to lift my precious noggin it stuck fast to the pillow. I was well and truly stuck. It was with considerable alarm that I grabbed my head with my hands and forcibly held it above my shoulders. I hadn't stepped five paces out of my front door before I began to attract the attention of the neighbours. The one redeeming factor was that I worked as a Wash Up Porter at the West Suffolk hospital. Instead of entering the staff door, I traipsed slowly toward the ER room, desperately clutching my bedraggled head. "What on earth have you done?'" were the cries of those who knew me as I passed on by. "I was head banging to Saxon and look I can't hold my head up," I whined dejectedly as I let go of my head and showed them how it dangled limply like a wilted flower. I heard a few snickers and a couple of good belly laughs as I plodded towards the A & E.

The diagnosis, surprise surprise, was severely strained neck muscles. The remedy was a whopping great neck brace. I tried desperately to blend in with the hospital wallpaper as I made my way up to the kitchens. As I traversed those long cold corridors, I bumped into Uncle Tom Cobley and all... porters, kitchen workers, nurses, and patients alike, all seemed to know exactly what had happened to me. There was a buzz going around about the youngster who had thrashed his head at a rock concert and could not hold it up.

"Ooh, look. That's him!" and "Whatever happened to you?" often from someone who had a gleam in the eye which screamed I know exactly what you did!

My ears that had been so numb the night before, now heard the giggles and snickers crystal clear, as I experienced the pain and embarrassment of my first guitar solo. It wasn't long before I refused to open my mouth and comment, but it was too late. Word had spread, fingers pointed and laughter cackled. I was still carrying my head, and wearing that neck brace, long after I had physically removed it from my body. It was one of those awkward, cringing and humiliating chapters that I wanted to forget, to bury in a box named do not disturb. That was until I scribed the following version of what truly went on that night.

FROM PAIN IN THE NECK TO:

KING OF THE CELTS

I am Andrew Steed. I am the great grandson of a Scottish Laird. I am named after the Patron Saint of Scotland and my full name means, 'The Strong High Spirited Horseman'. I am from the Isles; this land is in my blood. I am a descendant of the Davidson Clan, one of the original Clans of the Highlands. Our motto is 'Wisely If Sincerely,' our totem animal is the Stag. I am of the Innes bloodline also one of the original Clans of the Highlands. Our motto is 'Be Faithful' and our totem animal is the Boar. I also carry the blood of the invaders, the totem animal of the Lion roars inside of me in the form of the Daines clan from across the sea. I am a Steed, a spirited stallion and a magnificent mare. I am united to the horse, the totem animal that connects these Isles to Lady Sovereignty, to the land herself and to the High King who mates with the Horse Goddess for the prosperity of all.

I love these Isles, this magical land sings to me. I have traveled the length and breadth to hear her song. On a still summer's eve the apparent calm was a mask for what was yet to come. The battle drums were stirring. I had been alerted earlier in the day when a young warrior Rob Waters had crashed through my door with the news that the Saxons were invading. They had swarmed into the neighbouring town of the White Horse and their battle cries were taunting us.

I accepted the call to arms. Our war party gathered, we jumped on the wagon train thundering to the heart of the battle. The Saxons were there, a large war band clad in leather, smelling of sweat and alcohol. Their drums and drams fed their courage. Their leader took centre stage and called for all eyes to look towards his glorification. His ego thumped into our lines, his battle song was dominating the early skirmishes. We were not intimidated. I rushed, pushed, thrust my way to the frontline. In the pattern of all great Celtic warriors we swarmed our enemy. The chaotic charge into the heat of battle is what the Bards will sing of in our feasting halls. The initial rush is crucial and we all stampeded to be in the place of honour at the head of the line. My wild thrashing cut a path to the Saxon leader. I was in the heart of the action. I jostled for the right to face the foe eye to eye, to hold the centre, to be in the fury of their most deadly screams. My physical exploits in battle will be forever remembered. Their chief was shrieking and wailing his curses in my ear. His spittle rained down upon us. The screams of our foe were deafening. I could have fallen under such onslaught but I stood tall, swung my arm for all it was worth, plucked the bravado out of their war chants and I used my head. The head is the most valuable prize to us Celts; this cauldron of wisdom is the seat of the soul. I was after taking a memento home with me. Their heads would make mighty fine decorations; perhaps I would wear them across my chest. An almighty cheer rang out as the Saxons fled the field. We chanted for them to come back and the leader called his troops once more into the fray. It was a last surge. Their drums beat wildly, they strutted and strained and it was too little too late. A final scuffle before the inevitable flee.

By the end of the evening I had my trophy. I paid for it mind you. I was soaked in sweat and ready to pull on fresh garb. It felt good to hang the frozen faces of the Saxon Leader and his henchmen upon my torso. I would surprise a few people decorated with these. My exploits would not go unnoticed, I can tell you that!

When the Saxon voices dissipated in the night's mist, victory was ours, the blood curdling screams still ringing in all of our ears. My bed was a welcoming resting place after the exertions of the night.

When the sphere of life rose splendidly in the bright morning sky, I awoke to the sound of singing. I lifted my battle-bruised body off the bed, and held my head high and proud. When the gifted healers, our eminent druids and engaging bards saw me, they presented me with a tremendous gift. For my bravery, in honour of leading the line, I was presented with a golden torc. A renowned medicine man slipped it around my neck. As I walked through the feasting halls I heard the whispers. "That's him, he was the one that used his head. "All eyes upon me as I walked amongst my people. I took graceful steps, tall, erect, my long noble head held high. Everyone stopped and noticed as I strode regally past them. Many clambered for my attention, wanting me to retell the tale of my heroics. Many pointed at the torc, my story rippling like a wave through camp. The Bards spinning and weaving the tale until it reached dazzling proportions. People clustered whispering my name and sharing with bright grins about my dazzling exploits. The laughter and cheering echoed through the day. I was claimed a champion. As I walked so regally with my head held high, rumours spread that I was a Celtic King. I was 'The Strong

High Spirited Horseman' chosen to protect the land, mate with the White Horse Goddess, and become a King amongst Kings, a High King of the Celts!

EXCAVATING OUR STORIES

What fun I had taking what is essentially the same tale and putting a Celtic twist upon it. I laugh with the Universe at the threads that linked so perfectly in this story. The ancestors must have gathered with glee as I set off to watch a band named of all things 'Saxon' knowing one day that my life path would be called to know the Celtic stories and to fall in love with my own indigenous pathway. My guides were on it from the start, getting me to go to a gig to see a band that I did not like and then seeing to it that I bought a t-shirt!

The chunky neck brace that I was forced to wear becoming a golden torc was the icing on the cake. A torc, for those who are not familiar with the term, is a large stiff ringed necklace often ornately decorated with spirals or animal heads. Julia Jeffrey's painting majestically shows 3 torcs forged by the Smiths hands.

THE NEXT STEP; JOURNEY WORK AND/OR JOURNALING INTO A STORY

JOURNAL QUESTIONS

1. Look back through your life and find a situation/story that was challenging. Journal different perspectives from your wiser self's point of view and see what connections you can

make that bring a smile and/or laughter to your heart. What feelings need to be transformed from shadow to light? With this information you have the key elements to begin reclaiming a tale.

Using the example of moving from 'A Pain in the Neck' to 'King of the Celts' let's break down some of the key elements to see how I went from the original tale to the reclaimed version.

My friend knocks on my door – He becomes a young warrior.

The band Saxon that we were going to see – Perfectly named for the invading army that we were going to face.

The train journey – We join the wagon train.

The venue in Ipswich – I use the emblem of the football club, which is the White Horse an auspicious totem animal to the Gaelic and Brythonic tribes of these Isles as it represents Sovereignty, the goddess and the land.

The rush at the beginning of the concert as people jostled to see the band – I use this to describe the rush of battle. The Celts were famed for their initial battle charge.

The lead singer – Becomes the Chief or King of the Saxons.

The music – Becomes the war chants and the battle drums.

My head banging – I weave in the idea of the head being the seat of the soul and the vessel of wisdom. This is a huge part of Celtic culture.

Buying a t-shirt – This offers me the opportunity to talk as if I have claimed the heads of the Saxon leaders. It is known that the Celts would take the head of a worthy foe as a trophy. It was believed that by doing so you took the wisdom of that person with you.

The Doctors and Nurses – These become the Druids and Bards.

The neck brace – Becomes the Golden Torc.

My limited mobility with my neck and head – Becomes a regal walk fit for a King.

The point here is to allow the creative juice to flow. Let your imagination run wild. At the end of the day I know that the original story exists. However, by playing with the reclaimed version, I have shifted a pattern in the weave. I look at it differently and I feel it in a brand new way which shifts my perspective. There is no right or wrong here. It is all about creating a feeling inside of us that brings laughter, joy and healing into our being. At the end of this chapter I have given another example of how we can piece together a story from its original format into one that is ready and ripe for reclaiming. This offers further guidance to help get you started in reclaiming your own stories.

2. What does your name mean? Find out and journal how you have embraced the qualities imbued within each name. Knowing the meaning of your name is powerful. Are there aspects to the various meanings that can be found within each of your names that you fear and/or have difficulty embracing? If so why is this? What can your name teach you about yourself that you do not already know?

3. If you have family mottos what are they and how do they relate to your life? If you do not have a motto for one or more lines of the family create one that would honour that lineage. It would be fun to draw/paint/collage a crest with the motto emblazoned upon it or write a short story about how the motto was bestowed upon your family.

4. Journal where you have been banging your head against a brick wall? Take a look where you have followed the crowd and jumped into something that you knew was not for you that has ended up causing you pain. Out of this situation what did you learn that has helped you grow?

5. Choose bands, books or organizations that have influenced you and take a look at what aspects of nature are emblazoned in their emblems. Then write down the strengths and abilities of this aspect of nature and see how they are connected with you and your life. Research meanings from mythology, world culture as many places as possible. For example if I lived in the USA and followed the North American football team known as the Baltimore Ravens, I would work with the Raven. Perhaps you are an avid Harry Potter fan and you have a favourite house which would connect you to the lion, badger, snake or

eagle. If I had pictures or photos on my wall as a kid of a favourite player/singer/book character I would look up the meaning of their names and work with that as well.

Bonus Question
What question can you find to ask yourself from this chapter that has not yet been asked?

SHAMANIC JOURNEY WORK

1. Journey to a favourite place in nature that you frequented as a kid and ask your child self, your teen self and your adult self to join you. Ask them to show you a story/situation that would free up life space in you through the art of reclaiming. Ask for clear guidance of how you can move forward with this.
2. In the story King of the Celts I reveal my name means 'The Strong High Spirited Stallion'. Find out what your name means and then journey to your guides to see how you have embodied the aspects of your name. Ask them if there are areas that you have hidden/run away from in fear of owning the fullness of your own name.
3. Look to see if you have any family mottos in your ancestral story. Journey to an ancestral clan gathering and ask to be shown the full meaning of the motto and how you embody it in your life. Why was this motto chosen? If you do not have a motto go and find out what the ancestors believe it ought to be and see how this motto connects to your life story.
4. Journey to see where you are putting your neck on the line. Where is your ego pushing you into places where you are over stretching and hurting yourself and all other beings? Where is Spirit guiding you to take risks that support you and all life?
5. Take a look at the names of towns, villages, cities that you grew up in or frequented in your youth. Take a look at organizations that you were deeply affiliated with and see what aspects of nature are emblazoned in their emblems. Also do the same with favourite bands that you listened to and books that caught your imagination. Once you have found one that peeks

your curiosity journey to ask to be shown a deeper meaning that this aspect of nature has taught you in your life. What can you do to honour this aspect of nature in the future?

Bonus Question
What Journey can you offer yourself from exploring this chapter that has not already been suggested?

ANOTHER EXAMPLE

When I was 8 years old I went on a school trip to Chadacre Farm in Suffolk. I had a brand new coat on. As we traipsed through a farmyard gate I slipped and fell into a pile of cow dung and mud. I was covered in wet sloppy mud and poo. The boys and girls snickered; I went bright red and spent the rest of the day wandering around feeling smelly, dirty and foolish. As I look at this experience through my wiser self and apply the tale to my life today I find some juicy morsels to work with.

My key words are: 8 years old, school, Chadacre Farm, brand new coat, slipped, fell, cow dung, mud, snickered, bright red. The feelings that needed to be transformed are: Dirty, smelly and foolish. As I connect the tale to my life today the first word that springs out from my key words is cow dung.

Let's look at the word cow to begin with; I walk and work a Celtic shamanic pathway. The cow to the indigenous ancestors of these isles represents abundance and prosperity. The cow is also deeply connected to Brighid. It is said that a white cow with red ears that gave a never-ending supply of milk accompanied St. Brighid on her journey through life. Brighid is both a goddess and a saint who represents creativity and fertility and is a bridge connecting the pagan Celts to the Christian Celts.

Now for the word dung; whilst I wallow in the feelings of foolishness and I remain stuck being dirty and smelly I stay trapped in the story where all is crappy. However if I work with the dung and shift perspective the crap becomes fertilizer. It's all about transforming our crap to fertilizer.

Now let's play with the other words;

Mud; Many years ago a wise woman once followed me into a fogou, an iron age cave in Cornwall that may have been used for spiritual purposes or storage. The ground was churned up, the fogou leaked from the heavy rains and it was a mud bath. I had strolled into the darkness beyond expecting the group of pilgrims who were traveling with me to follow. When I turned around they were all clustered at the edge looking dismally at the mud. The wise woman pushed her way through and urged them to follow calling "Come on what are you afraid of, it's the Mother's blood."

8 years old; the number 8 represents infinity.

School; this was part of my education.

Brand new coat; my new coat represented a new skin that was about to be caked in the Mother's blood and fertilizer.

Chadacre Farm – The name Chad is from the Welsh 'cad' meaning battle. It is also named as a protector. Acre is an area of land or a field. So I was working on the Protective Farm in the Field of Battle!

Snickered; what if the snickers turned to laughter turned to cheers?

Bright red: My skin is pale white, I am so very Celtic, if you put me in the sun you had better cover me up. When I get embarrassed and turn red it beams off me. So my story has bright red and pale white within it. These are the colours of the underworld, of the fae and the colours of Brighid's faerie cow.

Slipped/Fell; in my story this will be a calling a literal pulling that takes me to kiss the earth.

With all of these connections a story that is part of my own spiritual journey is ready for the writing. In short it will be about how I traveled to a place of protection where I could go into the world and stand in my battle truth. Brighid called to me, marked me, birthed me in the Mother's blood and then fertilized me with the abundant medicine of the sacred white cow as my new skin soaked in her juices. She called to me to be educated in the old ways, pulling me onto my knees until I lay with my heart upon the land, to kiss the earth and be humble in front of my peers. I was to wear the colours of the underworld on my skin and to be blessed this way during my 8th year, the sign of infinity, marking my connection with Brighid forever. I was washed in her creative juices to carry the bundles of poetry, healing and smithcraft out into the world. Those that witnessed this calling pointed, some cheered and laughed in jubilation, others who did not understand the importance of the moment shook their heads in bafflement. As my cheeks burned red hot she branded me with the fire. On my return home I bathed in the waters to integrate both of the elements of fire and water that spring forth from her infinite wisdom.

I have taken the significant elements and transformed the shadow of the old story into the light of a new one. I am beaming inside at this new version. I giggle in delight. This transformational medicine works if we are prepared to work it. So you have a choice, you can skim the surface of these questions and wallow in your own muck or you can allow yourself to creatively explore and tend your own inner garden, it is your journey and those with courage will discover their own hero shining within.

Chapter 2

By the Strength in My Arm,
the Truth in My Heart
& the Promise on My Lips

This ancient Celtic saying rings true when it comes to the art of reclaiming. It will take strength to go beyond the surface and dive into our story. A pen feels weightless in the hand yet through this inky sword mighty words can be spilt on a page. We need strength to pick that pen up and wield it with a flourish to reclaim our tale. It means making a commitment, doing the work! It takes courage to look authentically into the heart of a challenging chapter and we need to trust the process. We need to trust in ourselves to creatively find the words or perhaps drawings that speak to the transformational change within the tale. In a nutshell, it means having the guts to take a look at our shadows.

A few years ago I was working in a high school in Pennsylvania. I remember a 16-year-old young woman who shook her head dejectedly. She struggled with putting voice to a reality that had bound her and held her for a number of years. It took immense courage for her to open up. This is true for each and every one of us. We need to feel safe and in part we need to trust those around us as we explore our stories. The ultimate trust is in ourselves, to be willing to let go, for it is each of us who has to do the work in the end. It was a deep-rooted shameful piece that had trapped her since birth. The first step she had to make to untangle these threads was to name them.

The thought that had been bound into her reality was that she was a 'mistake'. Her birth onto the planet was an error. It had been rammed home as a 'fact' by her parents. They had repeatedly told her that she was unplanned, a blunder on their

part. Even though they added they were glad that she was with them, the initial unintended pregnancy was the piece that hit home. It was the fact they called her an accident that took root, she bought into their perception. She had taken ownership of feeling unwanted, of being a burden, a mistake. At her core this young woman felt unworthy and unloved.

Interestingly I could have found myself wrapped in the same bindings. I remember in my teens the day my dad told me my brother was planned; I on the other hand was totally unexpected. I was an accident, the result of a night on the town, a case of one too many. Followed by a night of passion with no thought of contraception or the consequences and hey presto up I pop, or more to the point out I pop 9 months later! My response was along the lines of "well of course you didn't plan to have me, I chose you. It was my plan and I was ready so I came to work some things out with you as my parents." I am not sure where this idea sprouted. I just knew it was my truth, a truth that resonated in a place of deep knowing way inside of me. It was old knowledge and by voicing it and feeling the reality of it my whole being was empowered.

The young woman struggled with this concept initially. However she sat with it for some while. It was in the creative writing that this alternative reality freed something inside of her and she was able to totally shift her perspective. I received a letter from her about 2 months after in which she shared that she felt totally liberated. She was an athlete, part of the school track team, she was so excited to reveal that since she reclaimed her story her running times had dramatically improved. In choosing to own the perspective that she chose to be born into her family there was nothing holding her back, she was able to run much faster. It was a revelation to her and a confirmation to me that when we release something holding us hostage we have more freedom to fly.

WORD MAGIC

Words carry weight. They pack a punch. It is why lawyers introduce inadmissible evidence in court. When the judge tells the jury to disregard those statements it is too late, they have been made and to good effect. A journalist writes an article that decimates someone's character only to write a retraction in a later publication. The apology comes too late; the damning words have already taken hold. People tend to believe what they read. It is in print, it must be true. One of the reasons indigenous people did not write a thing down was that once you did it was fixed; they saw the beauty in the constant change and evolution within the story.

I have struggled with this aspect as a writer. I am sure most writers have, it is why we make so many rewrites. And yet I find value in both the written and the oral word. The written word conveys so many ideas and can reach people who pick up your book and feel a connection to what it is you are conveying even though you have never met in person. A bridge is built. Whether we are talking about the oral word or the written word, the key ingredient here is the thought. Our thoughts bind our reality. If we think it, so it is. What activates the magic, the transformational quality that breathes life into our words is feeling. The spoken words will only travel so far. Add emotion to them and we set things in motion. A saying that I have used many times when giving a motivational speech is, "It is not important what I say here today. You're thinking, 'It had better be, we have invested an hour/a day/a weekend with this guy,' yet what I say is not significant. What you think when I say it, that's what is important." I would add that it really is about what you add to those thoughts, your feelings around them. This is what gets you invested.

The old adage is 'Be careful what you wish for.' There are many grand 'wish' stories. One of my children's favourites growing up was about a girl named Matilda Alice. Matilda could be a really mean piece of work. She is granted 3 wishes by a magic toad for agreeing not to stomp upon its head. For her third wish she chooses to make her next 10,000 wishes come true. She then promptly drives over the toad squashing him in her brand new Ferrari sports car, which incidentally was her second wish. All is going sweetly for Matilda until she gets to school. One of her classmates asks if she has studied for an impending test. She screams about having forgotten and goes off on a rant. In her outburst she blames the toad for her predicament and carelessly wishes she were dead. And that was the end of Matilda Alice. This is a great reminder to pick our words carefully.

Our words and thoughts shape our lives. Several years ago a young woman came on pilgrimage with me to Cornwall, Somerset and Wiltshire. As we worked on what I commonly refer to as word magic she shared how accurate this information is. She had learned a hard sharp lesson in regards to word magic. She shared how she used to always say 'he/she/that is such a pain in my backside.' When she had made this statement she unconsciously added the feeling of anger and frustration to the mix. The combination of the words and the feelings resulted in her developing a cancerous growth in her rectum. It is not to say that when someone contracts a disease that they have done something wrong. She was just self-aware that when we focus our thoughts on something, the Universe looks to support our efforts. If we are able to look at what we have created in our lives without judgment we can begin to shift the energy. It is why reclaiming the story can be so powerful. As we sat on the Mump, a sister hill to Glastonbury Tor in Somerset, she disclosed that she was now in a state of remission and was incredibly grateful for having been introduced to the importance of setting clear goals to reclaiming her health.

What often stops so many of us in our tracks is leaving out the most vital step in reaching our goals. We dive into a project headfirst and take action making this the number one priority.

In actual fact the first step is having a clear picture, a plan, devised in our mind's eye, with us in the centre of the frame surrounded by what we are manifesting in technicolour, the more detail the better. Action is the third step and an imperative part in making sure things get done. Step two is the heart centre, the bridging place, it is where we pour and mix our feelings in to the brew. This phase is often overlooked and is the most vital stage of all. Our passion for the vision that we have painted needs the bonding agent, the magic, that initiates and drives the action for the project to reach fruition.

As I have explored this process I liken these 3 steps to how the ancient Celts saw the world. They worked with the number 3 and saw the importance of looking after our spiritual, mental and physical body. I believe for all of us there is a rich treasure trove beyond our wildest dreams sitting in the Spiritual waiting for us to activate it. The way for us to access the flow is through our feelings. To manifest from the Spiritual into the Physical we must cross over the Mental Bridge. When we feel worthy we give the Universe the green light that allows the wealth of our own spiritual gifts to flow generously into our lives. We each have a golden ticket to the richest tastiest feast so let's pull up a chair and dine from the banquet table rather than fighting each other for the scraps on the floor!

What words and feelings do we need to stir in our cauldron? Being willing to journey into our stories and reclaim them takes us out of victim and allows us to be in the rhythm with the hero in our lives. In working this heart magic we can delve into our imagination to reweave, reclaim, remember and recreate.

THE NEXT STEP: JOURNEY WORK AND/OR JOURNALING INTO A STORY

JOURNAL QUESTIONS

1. Where has your voice fallen silent in the world? Take a look at different areas/relationships in your life and journal where you feel your voice struggles to be heard. On the flip side,

where has your voice been overbearing in the world? Take a look at present situations/relationships and journal where you have been so busy putting across your opinion that you have overshadowed others. What change are you willing and able to make to listen more attentively and to be heard gently and powerfully in the world?

2. What have you ever released in your life that has given you a sense of freedom and the ability to fly? Is there something you would like to release now? Journal what your life might look like if you made this change.

3. Have you ever faced a time where you were accused of doing something you didn't and/or had a person believing something about you that was not true? Journal the key elements of this event and see how you can begin to reclaim it.

4. I often ask groups of people "Who do you talk to most in this world?" The answer is you. We are constantly yakking away inside our own heads. What sayings have crept into your daily vocabulary that does not support your well-being? What self talk is damaging your self-esteem right now? I advocate taking an internal shower as well as an external shower. We wash our bodies so we do not smell. Why not take the time to talk to self with empowering words. If you think you do not have time it is important to make time. Whilst in the shower, driving or riding in a vehicle on the way to work/school or before drifting off to sleep anytime is a great time to do this. I advocate implementing this for one whole week and keep a journal of your experience. Then add another week and so on until it becomes a healthy habit.

5. Take a look at one goal you would like to achieve and create a vision board around it. Put yourself in the centre of the picture and then close your eyes and fill up with the joy of having achieved it. Journal how this makes you feel. Hang the vision board where you can see it each day and go to it and tap into the feeling of achieving your vision each day for a week, then continue for another week and beyond. Your vision has already happened it is just waiting for you to catch up to it!

Bonus Question
What question can you find to ask yourself from this chapter that has not yet been asked?

SHAMANIC JOURNEY WORK

1. Journey to an ancestral hearth to talk with your ancestors ask to witness your own birth and see what tangled threads you brought in with you that connect to your ancestral line.
2. Journey to a trusted guide and ask them to take you into the treasure room of your own spiritual storehouse. What treasures are you ready to bring into the physical and how will this help the world by doing so?
3. Journey to a guide that works with your health and well-being. If you do not have a guide who takes on this specific role then I recommend that you journey first to find one who is willing and able to take on this role. Ask this guide to show you any places that you are creating disease in the world through careless use of your words that are infused with feeling.
4. Journey to a feast hall and take a look at where you and your ancestors have fought for the scraps on the floor. What kept them and possibly you from claiming your seat at the table? Invite them to join you and feast at the table.
5. Journey to see what can be released on a physical, mental and spiritual level that will allow you to fly with more freedom in the world.

Bonus Question
What Journey can you offer yourself from exploring this chapter that has not already been suggested?

Chapter 3

Honouring the Child Within

"The great person is one that does not lose their child's heart."
-Based on a quote by Mencius

As a child we are bombarded with messages that often crush our spirit. "Be quiet"; "Children should be seen and not heard"; Dummies or pacifiers shoved in a child's mouth so the adult can have some peace. Is it any wonder we have difficulty finding and owning our voice? Then there is this incessant race to 'grow up'. How many of us were told, "Why don't you grow up?" "Act your age"; "Don't be such a baby"; "Stop acting like a little kid." And all this whilst we were still little kids. One of the greatest gifts we can give ourselves is to let our inner child out and give them permission to play.

What did you love to do as a child that your adult self has walked away from? I love splashing in puddles, getting muddy, blowing and chasing bubbles, putting my bare feet on the earth and squishing mud or sand between my toes. I like to go on midnight walks, camp under the stars, climb trees and build faerie houses and outdoor dens. These are just a few of my childhood memories that I have carried into my adult years.

Oliver Wendell Holmes wrote, "Most people die with their music still in them," a statement that carries a huge amount of truth. So many people live in fear of being themselves. I believe that we all have symphonies yet to be discovered within us. The art of playfulness is key. Allowing our creative selves to join the party and celebrating this gift of life, our life and reveling in our unique story. The world becomes more magical when we look through soft eyes rather than hard stares. I give myself permission to express my true nature and dress in colours and clothes to suit my personality rather than society's idea of who I should be. I have always had a dress up box. What was once for special occasions has grown into my day-to-day attire.

As a child I was born to play. The woods were my backyard playgrounds, and my curious imagination was as fertile as the rich soil of my birthplace in East Anglia. I am to this day an adventurous free-spirited soul. In my early twenties I would often dress and encourage my friends to dress as a character from whichever book I was reading at the time. Hence we all dressed as hobbits, wizards, elves and dwarves and went in search of an old tower in a local wood whilst I was tackling the delights of Tolkien's *Lord of the Rings*. We became moles when I was engrossed in William Horwood's *Duncton Wood*. We went to a village pub dressed as old people all with mole names and specific mole characteristics. We then headed to an underground system of caves near Horringer Court on the outskirts of Bury St. Edmunds. We scampered through the caverns playing Blind Mole's Bluff before clambering through a derelict mansion that stood on a rise amongst the knolls and hollows of this tangled woodland. Then there was the time that we headed to Cornwall for the weekend dressed as Pirates and stormed St. Michael's Mount so we could call ourselves the Pirates of Penzance. My favourite though was dressing as Robin Hood. The Green Man is in my blood; I was desperately disappointed when I was overlooked for the part of Puck from Midsummer Night's Dream with the local Summer Theatre production in 1979, but nothing was going to stop me adorning myself as Robin of Loxley. I would do more than dress the part. I had decided to head to his stomping ground amongst the boughs and ferns of Sherwood Forest. Based on a true account I have whisked together a reclaimed version. I will describe my deviations and imaginative retelling anon.

THE TALE OF ROBIN HOOD AND HIS MERRY MEN

I never tired of the unique way Poppers started every time her engine was turned over. Poppers was my beloved little green car.

She was a 1960 Ford Popular, round in shape with little windows and such a lovable face. Oh yes, Poppers definitely had a face. She was a car with character and anyone who took the time to gaze into her eyes would be drawn to her beaming grin. This morning was no exception. I chuckled out loud as I pulled the tiny button that awoke Poppers from her slumber. "That's my girl!" I cried. "It takes more than a key to get your little heart pumping." She was a gem of a car and I loved her eccentricity. She needed to have a key inserted for her to start but it took the rapid movement of pushing a lever in and out to ignite her fire. Poppers and I shared several character traits, we both loved to smile, we were both a tad unconventional and we were both born in the 1960's.

I was the tender young age of 22. I had awoken that morning with three glorious days stretching before me. I had nothing on my plate, nowhere I had to be. I was free to follow my heart and go where the wind called me. As I stretched my lean body and rummaged through my drawers searching for the clothes that caught my eye I was struck with a bolt of inspiration. How about I adorn the forest green and step into the world as one of my all time favourite heroes Robin Hood? His rebellious

spirit was akin to my own. To provide sustenance to the poor and address the balance of the greedy aristocracy who looked down their noses at those they deemed unworthy. These noble qualities had always struck a chord in my heart. I dug around until I found a green shirt and an old tunic that had tinges of green and brown. It looked magnificent with a thick leather black belt wrapped around it. My long legs were camouflaged in green tie-dye leggings with a tatty ripped up pair of jeans pulled on top. I tugged on my beaten up leather army boots that laced up to my knee. The crowning glory was a home made two-tone green and bronze hat with a pheasant feather sticking out of the side. To complete the ensemble I tucked a small wooden sword inside my belt. I strolled into the bathroom and checked myself out in the full-length mirror. "Looking good," I giggled. I grabbed a sleeping bag, some supplies, my brolly tent that I used for fishing trips and jumped into Poppers.

It was certainly a beautiful day, sunshine, blue skies and puffy white clouds. I slid on my fluorescent green sunglasses beaming from ear to ear. My good friend Mark was going to get a kick out of me knocking on his door today. As Popper's engine purred I added my voice to the mix in a sweet rendition of "I can see clearly now the rain has gone. I can see all obstacles in my way. Gone are the dark clouds that had me blind. It's gonna be a bright, bright sun-shining day."

The smell of adventure was hanging thick in the air. I was bursting with chuckles as I climbed out of Poppers and marched towards Mark's back door. His face was a picture when he opened it. His eyes were on stalks. "What on earth are you up to?" He inquired quizzically.

"I'm Robin Hood," I beamed.

"I can see that, but what are you up to?"

"Well it's like this," I began, "I thought I'd drive up to Nottingham and sleep in Sherwood Forest."

"Wicked," sniggered Mark, "let me grab my gear."

About twenty minutes later, Mark emerged in old boots, ripped up jeans, a shabby leather cut off jacket, a thick belt with a large bronze buckle, a couple of leather shoulder bags, and a rustic hat adorned with a bright red feather. Mark had olive skin, long dark dread locks, deep brown magnetic eyes, and though he was small boned, he had a strong chiseled jaw, high cheek bones, and an elfin smile that could capture your heart in a beat. He was a man that I loved, a blood brother, a kindred spirit and a willing playful soul who was game for stepping out onto a quest.

"Do I look the part, or do I look the part?" He asked, knowing full well that he looked the part. He walked with an air of confidence; his spindly five foot six frame always seemed so much bigger.

"You're too much Mark," I teased. "That's it, I'm Robin Hood and you're Much." He eyed me curiously and then chuckled as I added, "Much the Miller, one of Robin's Merry Men." Our laughter was still echoing in my ears as we paid a call on our pal Johnny.

Johnny was a slender built young man in his early twenties. His striking features were his naturally blonde wavy hair, which looked all the more prominent when he blushed, and he blushed frequently.

"You look like Robin Hood," He stammered as he peered out the doorway.

"I am Robin Hood. Mark's Much the Miller and we are headed to Sherwood. Fancy coming?"

"Who shall I be?" he croaked expectantly.

"Put on your sister's dress and you can be Maid Marion!" Mark cackled playfully. Johnny's face turned boozy red. "Only kidding," joked Mark "You can be Will Scarlet." With his face glowing hotter than the embers of a fire Johnny was a dead ringer for Will Scarlet.

Johnny quickly rooted through his drawers, and with our help, was transformed into an odd looking Will Scarlet. Army boots, jeans, with a red bandana hanging out of the back pocket, a red polo neck, black cut off jacket, and a red beret with a wild turkey feather pinned on the side. He grabbed a gnarled walking stick to act as his trusted staff and we settled ourselves in Poppers and headed north.

Nottingham from Bury St. Edmunds is close to a three-hour drive in a regular car. Poppers was no ordinary car. She balked at going over 50 miles an hour. When she went up hill in the rain the windscreen wipers squeaked across the screen going really, really slowly, when she went down hill they flashed across the window as if there were no tomorrow. Poppers was my trusted steed. She wasn't fast, but she was reliable. Slow and steady she took us all the way to Sherwood.

Mark and Johnny and I were in our element. We strolled around the forest as if we owned it, yet we were careful to hide from prying eyes. "Quick boys take cover, I think I hear the sheriff's men!" I cried and we scampered off into some undergrowth. The game was on, the task was to remain unseen. We dodged in and out of the shadows, crept silently along unmarked trails tracking innocent parties of visitors through the ancient woodland of Sherwood. Occasionally when spotted we swiftly dove behind a bush listening to comments like, "Did you see that? I swore I just saw Robin Hood."

When we finally rested it was at a most fitting place. In the heart of the forest is a mighty oak that is hollowed out. It is said that inside this tree Robin and the Merry Men would gather. So it was on a fading summers eve in 1985 that Robin, Much and Will retraced their ancestral footsteps.

"This is wicked," grinned Mark.

"Yeah but we'd better make tracks if we want to find a camping spot for the night."

"I saw a sign for a campground on the main road," declared Johnny as we headed towards Poppers.

"I don't know about you, but I want to sleep here in the forest." My eyes lit up as the Merry Men nodded their heads in agreement.

As if the heart of the forest was calling us a deer appeared and ran down a trail. It was a sign; we would head that way. The humpty bumpty rickety rackety track was just big enough for Poppers to fit down. I turned the key, pumped the starting button, turned Poppers' wheel and we chugged along the unmarked trail that led us off into the unknown. A rabbit darted across our path and we took it for another sign and pulled Poppers over. I eased her to a stop on the crest of a small hill, a perfect place to make camp. We had reached the gloaming so we speedily put up my little tent. A canvas thrown over a fishing umbrella that made a little round house. Our small domed tent was decorated with a small altar that burned three candles upon a colourful Indian tablecloth, over the door we hung wild flowers and inside we scattered colourful patchwork blankets. It was our humble abode for the night and we greedily tucked into the picnic that I had packed in Popper's boot.

"Real gypsy stylie, looks wicked." Mark smiled triumphantly. I had to agree, it had a certain rustic charm about it. As much as we would have liked to have a fire, we decided it would be too challenging to collect firewood in the dark so we huddled around the glow of candlelight peering into the blackness of the night. The forest was still. An occasional rustling of leaves could be heard. The witching hour approached. The moment was ripe for a ghost story or something that went bump in the night. That was when the dragon roared. A huge rumbling shattered the silence, two massive eyes burning bright, shining and glaring directly towards us. The growling beast was coming closer and closer. It was a Land Rover. Someone was driving a vehicle in the middle of the forest past the pumpkin side of midnight.

When it was less than 100 yards away, the engine was cut and the blinding lights flickered into darkness. Immediately we extinguished the candles. Whoever was in the vehicle was not making a move. They were sitting tight. Mark and Johnny and I were like slabs of granite, frozen to the spot waiting the unfolding of this eerie drama. Still no one moved. Seconds turned into minutes. My heart was pumping yet I was hardly breathing, not daring to shatter the tense silence for fear of what might happen. Another minute passed, a minute that seemed like a painful lifetime. They were sitting in the dark as we were sitting in the dark, they were sitting in the dark as we were sitting in the dark, and they were sitting in the dark as we were sitting in the dark. I could bear it no longer.

"What are we going to do?" I whispered.

"You're Robin Hood, you check it out," hissed Mark.

So I stood tall and carried my lanky self towards the parked vehicle. As I took action it all felt surreal. There I was stepping into the silence of the night as Robin Hood in deep dark Sherwood walking towards who knows what with a wooden sword swinging at my hip. The cheerful grin was about to be wiped off my face. Blinding headlights flashed into my eyes, then in unison the doors to the jeep were thrown open. I blinked fiercely. Spots of light dancing on my horizon obscuring my vision, I shook my head desperately trying to refocus. Out of the darkness two large shadows honed in on me.

"Get down, get down!" a gruff guttural roar cracked me from my stillness and sent shivers down my spine. "Get down, I say, get down!" Now I don't know about you but I love to get down. Dancing is one of my favourite things but this was no nightclub and I was certainly not being invited to strut my stuff. A fleeting image of my legs being stuck to the spot as in some of my worst nightmares was swept aside as survival instincts took over. Running at full speed through an unknown forest in the dark is not the most sensible thing to do. However having looked into the demonic eyes of a raging madman closing in on you whilst wielding a club wildly above his head will stir something in you. As he dashed my way I hurtled off at full pelt. I could feel him closing and swung my body desperately away from the impending blow. I heard the swish of the stick that whipped through the air behind me. I was quick but not quick enough. A sturdy thwack, the sound of wood striking flesh reverberated in the midnight air. The force of the blow knocked me to my knees, I lunged forward and in utter desperation scrambled and clawed my way through the undergrowth. There was a second strike, the club whistled through the air and this time its song stuttered in a tremendous splintering crash. The club snapped in two as it shuddered against the firm trunk of a mighty oak. I did not stop to see what had happened next. I fled as fast as my shaking legs would carry me.

Lost, alone, afraid and in pain, I tried to gather my thoughts. I wandered in a dream state, a walking waking nightmare. I was Robin Hood and I was lost in Sherwood. What now? I dared not call out in fear of the repercussions. Then I heard the snap of a branch breaking underfoot. Someone was coming my way. Was it friend or foe? I stood motionless my breathing heavy from the terror of the ordeal. I prayed vehemently that it was Mark or Johnny. The footsteps came close and out of the misty moonlight stepped a foe. His voice was shrill as he stammered, "Don't run, stay where you are."

It was not the gruff raw voice of the club wielding Sheriff of Nottingham. This voice was tense, strained with an element of fear. It was the Sheriff's sidekick. However the Henchman's next words brought no immediate reassurance. "You are safe, no one's going to hurt you."

Like I believe you I thought. "What do you want?" I fired back slowly edging my way into the woods getting ready to flee for all I was worth.

"To take you back to your friends, that's all," coaxed a heavyset young man in his early twenties. The moon had come from behind a cloud and shone into the clearing. I frantically scanned the clean shaved ruddy face of the approaching man and stared right into his eyes. Something in his troubled gaze spoke to me and I felt a surge of trust. There appeared to be no malice in him. He looked as shaken as I was.

"Okay, let's find them, I'll follow you," I nodded cautiously.

"Don't worry, no one's going to hurt you" was his constant call. I was just starting to believe him, when I caught sight of the Sheriff who was fighting with yet another oak tree. His rough hands pulling and pushing one of the thinner branches, then with the aid of a machete he hacked the limb free. He was replacing the broken staff that had shattered when he had looked to bludgeon me. To my indignation he proceeded to bash my tent. Mark and Johnny were decidedly not merry. They both crouched dismally behind a bush. We were all as pale as ghosts. I watched in dismay as my tent collapsed with each clumsy swing of the Sheriff's new club and a sudden breeze of courage gained by outrage toward the situation surged through my veins.

"Oi, that's my tent" I barked.

"Shut your mouth!" growled Nottingham "I clubbed you once and I'll club you again. Where are your guns, where are your traps? I'll teach you to poach from this land."

"We don't have any, look all I've got is a wooden sword. I'm Robin Hood, I...I..."

"If you're Robin bloody Hood, then I must be the Sheriff of flipping Nottingham," jibed the bearded giant.

If I hadn't been in such a precarious position, I would have agreed that indeed he was the Sheriff of Nottingham. The Sheriff lifted his new club high into the air and was about to rain it down for another canvas-ripping swing when everything changed.

Stillness flooded over the forest. It was an eerie quiet that sprouted goose pimples across my skin. It was if the spirits of the dead were watching us, as if Robin Hood had returned to protect his own. Within a heartbeat the wind picked up, a forceful blast shrieked through the forest. The trees danced and twisted with the swift gust of air. Their limbs grabbing like arms, searching out the evil within their midst. It was so strong it nearly knocked me off my feet. Whipping and whirling, the mighty oak that had fallen foul to the Sheriff's knife swing claimed retribution for its torn off limb. It reached out and snatched at him with a flailing branch. It snagged itself into his belt, and at that very moment, the tempest was silenced. With no wind, the trees that had been bent double shot back upright standing noble, tall and strong. As they whipped up to their full height the Sheriff went shooting up in the air. There he hung, his flaying squat body dangling thirteen feet off the ground. Caught fast by his leather belt he swung panic-faced and squawking like a chicken. The Henchman stood below with his mouth open gawping at his boss. When he finally managed to squeak out some words it was a timid call of, "What do I do?"

We knew exactly what we were going to do. Within minutes Poppers was loaded and ready to go. I inserted the key, pumped the button that ignited her heartbeat and we drove merrily off by the light of the moon. In our rear view mirror I saw the Sheriff's henchman struggling to lower Nottingham from his lofty perch. With a resounding cheer we left our foes behind us. Once again Robin Hood escaped from the Sheriff of Nottingham!

EXCAVATING OUR STORIES

This story is based in truth up to the point of the Sheriff's club snapping. He did take a swing at me shouting "Get down" and he caught me squarely across my back with his walking stick. I nearly went to ground. I managed to stay on my feet to flee into the forest. I was pursued and found by his frightened henchman. When we returned to Mark and Johnny, the Sheriff was clubbing my tent. He thought we were poachers and it took a while to convince him that we were not. The nearest thing we had to a trap was my wooden sword. We hastily packed our belongings and were escorted out of Sherwood. We sat up most of the night at a nearby campground reliving this bizarre experience. The one thing that kept coming to me was Robin Hood just got beat up by the Sheriff of Nottingham. It went against every Robin Hood tale that I had ever heard. It desperately needed a rewrite! In later years I re-entered Sherwood and my imagination constructed this version. I like the new story so much more. Having the ghosts of Sherwood, the ancestors, return as my allies and the Sheriff dangling from the tree with his henchman all a fluster, brings a whopping great smile to my whole being. As I constructed an ending in which Robin Hood escaped I realized that I could revisit any of the challenging stories in my past and rewrite them.

"That's not the truth" I hear some of you say. Technically you are right. I have stretched the canvas and created a tall tale version of events. The reclaimed story in tall tale format is powerful. I cannot change my past; all I can do is change how I view it. This is a huge piece of medicine. Choices, choices. We can dig in our heels, be technically right and be forever stuck in the story. I prefer to sprinkle some imagination dust, stir in some belly laughs and compose an ending that tickles my fancy and delights my soul.

The great news is the art of reclaiming is available to us all. This process is inclusive. We can all do it. Another saying I have used often in motivational seminars is, "None of us are born winners or losers, we are born choosers." We are empowered through our ability to choose. We either become intimately involved in our own healing that promotes more life fuel, or we give away our power and coast into a semi-comatose existence. We don't have to carry the hopelessness of defeat like a millstone around our neck. We can break loose and let out our inner hero! It requires us to touch into our playful selves. Do you have a story that can be reclaimed through the guise of a fictional or *'his'torical character? You will know that the story has been reclaimed when you feel lighter in your heart and you can laugh with the story rather than at it. My feeling is when my story has been reclaimed I have shed like the snake, transformed like the butterfly, and my heart is shining golden rays that bridge the worlds between the worlds.

THE NEXT STEP: JOURNEY WORK AND/OR JOURNALING INTO A STORY

JOURNAL QUESTIONS

1. Let your imagination float through time and space to moments in your childhood where you were out in nature or were in the height of creativity and journal several moments that made you smile. Which of these situations call you to revisit and implement more often in your life?

2. If you could wear the hat and cloak of any storybook or 'his'torical character for the day whose robes would you wear and why? How are you like this character? What traits of this character could you imbue into your life story for the benefit of all?

3. Walking into the large oak tree where the legendary Robin Hood once planned adventures is like walking through a portal into another world. Where have you stepped through a doorway that led you to imagine yourself in a different world and/or where have you been surprised by walking into a situation that you thought would offer one thing and it offered something totally different? Work with something that shifted your perspective.

4. Take yourself out into nature for at least an hour, preferably longer. Find somewhere to sit where you are not around any other human beings. Allow your self to sit still and blend in with your surroundings. Listen to what the natural world has to say. Whether you choose a forest, river, mountain, lake, cliff edge or meadow, become a witness and notice insects, animals, clouds, sunlight, raindrops, shadows, the breath of the wind, and whatever else comes your way. Be silent, be still, and on your return journal what you learnt about yourself, your day, your surroundings, your life.

5. In the story the roar of the Land Rover makes us jump and then we sit in the dark wondering what is out there waiting for us. In the end I stood up and went to face the darkness. Where have you stood up and faced your fears? Journal about a time you found courage to face the unknown.

Bonus Question.
What question can you find to ask yourself from this chapter that has not yet been asked?

SHAMANIC JOURNEY WORK

1. Journey to your child self and ask how you can honour your own journey and the planet by playing more in and with the natural world.
2. Journey to a dress up box and open it up to see what fictional or 'his'torical' character's dress attire is inside. What characteristics do you share with this person? What aspects of this person's character could you imbue into your life story for the highest good of all beings?
3. In the story we enter the hollowed out oak tree that Robin Hood and the Merry Men used to gather in. Journey to the Spirit of the forest and ask to merge with an ancient oak. In the Celtic world oak is known for wisdom. Ask the tree to share oak wisdom with you. What seeds can be planted in your own life that will serve the wild places in the world?
4. When we arrive at Sherwood we run around the forest looking to be part of the unseen world. Journey to the Unseen beings in the forest and ask for a guide to wander in the forest with that will help you to cloak yourself and move unseen into the mysteries of an ancient forest. What are the essential secrets that are revealed in these wild places that will help you to strengthen your relationship with the green world?
5. In the story I am forced to confront whatever lies in wait for me in the darkness. Journey to your forest guide and ask them to support you as you face up to what dark shadows are in your life right now. What are you blindly running away from? Ask for support and guidance to carry your light into these dark spaces.

Bonus Question.
What Journey can you offer yourself from exploring this chapter that has not already been suggested?

- If there is a 'his'tory then surely there must be a herstory!

Chapter 4

In the Blink of an Eye

This next reclaimed story is in the same format and carries an added bonus. It shares again how weaving in a tall tale format frees the teller from his or her own original blueprint. It will also highlight the benefits of being released from the web of someone else's story. I am sure we all know someone who 'witnessed' the event and revels in bringing up the incident. I am sure that

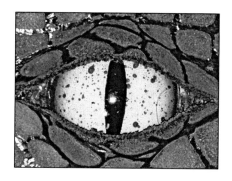

we all have a story that makes us cringe, one that is a guaranteed cause for embarrassment. Through reclaiming we shift our perspective. The taunts that would have picked bloody a scab of old find only a scar of a fully healed wound. Let me share an example of this with you.

THE RACE

In 1984 I was 21 and I lived in Upton Park, the heart of the East End of London. I rented an attic room in a house where supposedly 8 other people lived. In reality we had an average of 13 people staying there at any one time. I remember coming into the front room one morning and finding a bedraggled man in his mid twenties watching the T.V. I had no idea who he was. It later transpired that nobody else in the house knew him either. Beings he was from Newcastle we called him Geordie, on account of his accent. He stayed for about two weeks before disappearing one day. He left the place just as he had found it, chaotic, messy, but intact.

One Saturday night sticks firm in my mind from those reckless days. Come Saturday night the house would be buzzing by 10 pm and then the door would slam shut and silence would reign. It was then that we'd all empty onto the streets to hit the city pub and club scene. We'd dance the night away until the wee hours. No one stayed home on a Saturday. Yet on this particular Saturday night, one of the tenants Susie had stayed home. Susie was a go-getter, a saleswoman, vibrant, lively and never a hair out of place. This night she was unrecognizable, her eyes bloodshot and swollen, her nose red raw, her hair sticking up and out in all directions. She shuffled from the kitchen towards her room clutching a hot water bottle and a steaming hot cup of tea. A bad dose of the flu sent Susie to her bed.

It was 3.30 am when we dragged the festivities home. Fourteen merry souls staggered up Alcott Street to our front door. The house was in absolute darkness. The first sign that we were in trouble was on the doorstep. We all stood there waiting for the next person to fumble around and find a key. As the seconds ticked by it became apparent that no one had the foresight to have taken one. It was absurd. All the people who officially lived there were huddled up in the doorway glaring at each other with incredulity. A look that screamed, "Surely you remembered to bring a key." Fortunately we had back-up. Susie was tucked up fast asleep in a back room. We hammered on the door to wake her. It appeared we had more chance of wakening the dead that night. We certainly woke some of the neighbours. We pounded, battered and thumped on the door but it remained silent and dark within.

Now the only other doorway into the house was accessed through our back garden. The great news was this door was always left unlocked. What a simple solution you're thinking; unfortunately not. You see, the only way into our garden was to go through sixteen other gardens. We were in the middle of a long line of row homes all with fenced-in gardens. Making matters worse our house backed on to another set of row homes with the same set up. The only easy access to the garden was from inside the house. The alternative entrance was to scale a bunch of fences between 6 and 8 feet tall.

My best friend Mark and his older brother Paul accompanied me to do the dirty work and open the door. You have already met Mark from the Robin Hood story. He reminded me of a wood sprite. You may recall he stood about 5 foot 6 inches tall with a magnetic smile. He was always up for an adventure and hauling ourselves over fences in the middle of the night seemed by far the better alternative than standing on the doorstep.

Mark often boasted that he could have been an Olympic athlete. He was certainly fast and to my chagrin he always beat me in a race. So when he turned to Paul and I and mischievously yelled "Race you," my heart sank. The feeling of defeat clogged my nostrils and sat heavy on my chest. I regarded myself as fit and agile and, although not a sprinter, I was great at distance running. Mark was off for glory, he knew he would get to be the one to let the waiting crowd in and receive the accolades for doing so. As the word "Go" struck the air I hurled myself at the first wooden fence for all I was worth.

I was taller than Mark which by the third fence counted for something. I had a real glimmer of hope in my heart. Maybe what I lost on the ground I could gain in the air. We were neck and neck. Paul who was a lot heavier than both of us was already struggling. It was a betting cert that he'd tag in last.

"I'm gonna win this one, watch my heels!" I cried out gleefully

"In your dreams," Mark jibed.

I was determined that I would win; I'd show Mark, I'd show them all. At the halfway point I had pushed out in front. As we came towards the home stretch there was daylight or, should I say, moonlight between us. With three more fences to jump I took the luxury of a full look behind me. Mark was struggling, I was clearly ahead; I was going to win.

I grabbed the next fence and launched myself towards my triumph. Oh the sweet smell of victory. I was flying, I was flowing, feeling fresh, the sweet smell of success imbued in my nostrils. Splash!...... I would have screamed, but the shock of the cold water enveloping my body, froze my mind. I plunged into freezing darkness. Murky pond water engulfed me. The shock of having icy water surge up my nose panicked me. The pond was deep, as deep as a swimming pool and I didn't do swimming pools. Having my head under water terrified me. I sunk into the slimy muddy bottom and in my desperation I freaked. My long thin arms thrashed wildly struggling searching for something solid to grab on to. My legs kicked frantically trying to push my body upwards towards the safety of fresh clear air. My hands wrapped around the slimy foliage sprouting from the Pond's bed. Strangling water plants wove around my flaying body until I was immobilized. I was stuck fast and rapidly running out of breath. I searched for help. Where was Mark? Couldn't he see me? I couldn't see him, I couldn't even see my way to the pond's calm surface.

"You're stuck," gurgled a voice. With every ounce of strength I twisted my head urgently scanning for the voice of my saviour. There was no one there. A goldfish flicked its tail and disappeared from view. "Help me please," my mind screamed. I had to breathe; I was going to burst. Then I saw a light. A beam of golden firelight sparked a momentary hope in my heart. Then fear took me into its grip. I felt a wave of nausea flood through my body. I sat looking into the fixed fiery eyes of the largest snapping turtle I had ever seen. His piercing glare bored menacingly into my petrified brain. His mouth opened as if he was going to try and swallow me whole. Then he kicked towards me swimming ominously closer. He bore down quick and hard and I did the one thing that you never do when under water. I screamed. I opened my mouth in sheer terror. My muted cry gurgled silently in the on rush of water. The last remnants of breath knocked clear of my body as darkness rushed in.

"Andrew, wake up, are you okay?" Mark slapped my face and jerked my body. With my cheek stinging I coughed and spluttered and looked up at his wry smile.

"What...How?" My thoughts were reeling, what on earth had happened? As I lay there allowing my breathing to centre I realized Mark had pulled me free. "Thanks Mark, I think I would have drowned if you hadn't pulled me out. I..." I didn't get any further because Mark butted in.

"What? I didn't pull you out. When I jumped the fence you were sprawled out on the grass, soaking wet. You must have pulled yourself out. I was worried for a moment but then you puked up some water and..."

I don't recall what Mark said after that; my mind was changing gears yet again. How had I gotten out? I don't think Mark saw him. It was the flash of fire that caught my eye. There sitting by the pond with plant roots in his mouth was the giant turtle. Had he nibbled through my bindings? He looked at me and winked. His left eye glinted with sparks of firelight, then he dove into the water and I never saw him again. "Did you see that?" I yelled incredulously. "I see that you fell in the goldfish pond," roared Paul as he busted up in laughter strolling over to join us.

It no longer seemed to matter who won the race. The three of us climbed the final fences with my friends in sporadic palpitations of laughter whilst I was in a daze. When we finally reached the back door a throng of curious faces turned to greet us. Susie had heard the banging and everyone had sprawled in. The house, alive with the sound of lively conversation and music, stilled momentarily as Mark announced my entrance.

"Ladies and gentlemen through hell and high water we have journeyed. We climbed over high peaks, braved the darkness of the night and have returned smelling of fishpond. Put your hands together for Paul, for myself and for our brother-in-arms, the one and only 'Sharky Steed.'" To applause and laughter I climbed the stairs still in a fog of thought.

I stank of pond water. Mark ran a steaming hot bath for me. As I pulled off my sopping clothes Mark poked his head around the door fighting back the urge to burst into another fit of laughter. He nodded his head emphatically and said, "You know you proved me wrong. You were faster than me tonight. I was beat, and thanks for the lesson."

"The lesson?" I interjected.

"Look before you leap Sharky, look before you leap!" He grinned. I couldn't swear on it for sure, maybe it was just a trick of the light, but for a fleeting instance I swear I saw a gleaming fiery glow emanate from Mark's left eye, and then he winked at me.

EXCAVATING OUR STORIES

I have had so much fun with this reclaimed tale. I have shared it with countless audiences. The oral version is a joy to tell; there are so many great opportunities for animation. Being stuck in the pond with the snapping turtle coming towards me is a treasured moment. This story is based on a life event during my college days living in London.

That fateful night happened as I have written it right up until I hit the water of the goldfish pond. Oh, I fell in all right. I soared over the fence in glorious jubilation, the scent of victory a heartbeat away. Well so I thought. It all came to a soggy end with me landing in a garden pond. I was sitting in it as first Mark's head popped up, then Paul's. The two of them were in hysterics. We trudged back to the house and indeed Susie had been roused from her slumber. I took a ribbing, felt incredibly embarrassed and wanted nothing more than the earth to swallow me whole.

When I discovered reclaiming, this one was ripe for the picking. The introduction of the Turtle, a guardian power animal, changed everything. So much so that when I bumped into Paul recently and he dredged up the story I found the largest chuckle in remembering the event with a newfound twist. Here lies a wonderful gift. Once you have shifted your perspective you are no longer tied into the original blueprint. When someone fires a cringe-worthy moment at you instead of hanging your head in shame you can find genuine laughter. The old threads of ridicule have been replaced by cords of power. Plugging into the reclaimed version adds humour, light, freedom and a host of valuable lessons to our journey.

THE NEXT STEP; JOURNEY WORK AND/OR JOURNALING INTO A STORY

JOURNAL QUESTIONS

1. Journal on a time where you rushed into something without stopping to look at the consequences that caused chaos in your life. Here lie the bones for reclaiming a story.

2. Journal about a time where you have celebrated a victory before you reached your destination. Where did you take your eye off the goal? What could you learn from this incident that when applied to a current life situation would benefit you and others?

3. I landed in a gold fishpond when I threw myself towards victory. The pond was my rabbit hole, the turtle my white rabbit. Let your imagination out to play and create a scenario whereby you leap across the fence and land somewhere unexpected. Which animal do you meet? Do not spend ages thinking about this, go with what comes and then take a look at both the place you landed and the animal you meet. Look for the challenges and gifts that this encounter offers in your own life. Look up the qualities of the animal and reflect them to your own life experience.

4. Take a look at the gifts that the seasons bring where you live right now. Which is your favourite season and why? What gifts do each season bring? How are you like your favourite season? How are you like your least favourite season? Looking at the gifts of the seasons, what could you do differently to bring your own life into balance with the lessons gleaned from the natural world? You could also frame this question around the daytime, night-time and the betwixt and between.

5. We have all forgotten sometimes to take our key with us. We have locked ourselves out of something or somewhere. In reality we have solutions within us; we have a key tucked inside. Journal on what key/talent/gift/skill you have in you that you have not brought out and used lately. How could you take this key and work with it to open up some new doorways in your life?

Bonus Question.
What question can you find to ask yourself from this chapter that has not yet been asked?

SHAMANIC JOURNEY WORK

1. Journey to visit a wise turtle and ask where we are rushing through life desperately trying to win? Where are we putting ourselves into unnecessary competition and throwing our energies into areas that do not serve for the highest good?

   Turtle medicine is profound. The turtle in some nations is a trickster. The First People of what we now know as the USA and Canada call this land Turtle Island. It is said in a creation story that turtle dove deeper than any other being to return with earth upon its back. This earth became a sphere for life the Great Mother that we call home today. The Cherokee nation will tell you that the turtle nation carries a calendar upon their back. The 13 full moons of the year are represented by the 13 large squares etched into the main shell with approximately 28 to 31 small squares completing the border around the edge. The blue moon that often falls within the year completes the thirteenth moon. Turtle offers transformation, moon energy, a way to carry our home with us wherever we go, to travel lightly in the world. Turtle knows the value of going within contracting into its shell reminding us to journey into the darkness and visionary world. Turtle teaches us to sit with self and as many species of Turtle hibernate so we are called to remember to go through our own seasons. There is a time and place for all. How are we honouring the spring, summer, autumn and winter in our own lives? It is imperative we expand and we contract. Turtle is an ally to swim with in the underworld and also to walk with on land, teaching us how to adapt to change.

2. Journey to the spirit of the seasons and ask where am I out of alignment with my spring, summer, autumn, winter. What can I implement to honour the seasons in my life and how do I carry this wisdom out into the world?

3. In this story I am the one who ends up with egg on my face. I reclaim the story so that this 'egg' offers an opportunity for rebirth. I am reborn through the shapeshifting shamanic encounter with the Turtle.

Journey to a water guide. I work with Brighid who in the Celtic tradition is a midwife; she is a great ally. If you do not have a relationship with a water guide she is a great one to work with. Ask her/or your water guide to bring clarity to what needs transforming in your life right now. Ask to be supported in the birthing process to make this change. What do you need to do to help sustain this change for the fruits of change to grow?

4. Journey to the spirit of water and ask where am I drowning in a murky pool of my own making? Where have I jumped into a situation without looking that is causing unnecessary fear and panic in my life? What can I do to free myself from this fear?

5. Turtle is a great transformer. Evoking the spirit of turtle into my reclaimed story brought a fire of creativity that helped me to look at my own journey. It brought up questions such as where am I looking out for myself and for others? What gifts are hidden under the surface?

Journey to the spirit of creativity and ask what tools and treasures do I have hidden in my own tool bag that are being under-utilized and unused in my life. How would these tools benefit all beings if I were to get them out and utilize them?

Bonus Question.
What Journey can you offer yourself from exploring this chapter that has not already been suggested?

So how are you getting on with reclaiming your own stories? Have you put a spin or twist on any of them yet? Enjoy being the hero, revel in the role of trickster, discover wisdom from power animals, shape shift and solicit tears of joy as the lovable rogue. Whatever helps to heal, go for it with a passion and play, play, play!

Chapter 5

The Dark Knight & The Bright Day

Be grateful for whoever comes,
because each guest has been sent
as a guide from beyond.
Rumi.

So far we have looked at reclaiming a story using the key elements and weaving a tale around them. We have worked with a tall tale version and introduced a Power Animal to the mix. This time I will reclaim a challenging story by writing it as I remember it warts and all. To release the ghosts of the past we sometimes have to spill all of the shadows on to the page and in so doing we feel liberated in the sharing. When I put this story onto paper I found that I did not need to change anything. The sheer act of sharing brought total liberation and reclamation in itself.

ALL THINGS BRIGHT AND BEAUTIFUL...

The bus trundled along a winding lane where hedgerows grew tall and wild-flowers peeked out from every crevice. Cornwall is famous for its colourful slate walls dotted throughout the countryside. Anticipation kissed the air with a buzz of excited chatter amongst the members of St. Peter's Choir. We were nearing the towering spires of Truro Cathedral, the working destination of our annual holiday experience. We were staying in the grandeur of a sixteenth century mansion for the duration of our stay.

That sunny August morning I had climbed aboard and chosen a window seat. I had pressed my face to the glass and waved furiously until the figure of my mum was no longer in sight. I was 11 years old, skinny as a rake and a wide-eyed innocent. I was part of a motley crew of thirteen boys, nine men, an old granny who was to act as our chaperone and the ominous Choir Master, Mr. Bellows. He was well named, for his legendary rants had brought many a choirboy to the verge of tears.

This was the third time I had ventured from the safe haven of my family nest. I had visited Wales on a school trip and had made the same trek to Cornwall with the choir the previous year. My older brother who had since left the choir had accompanied me then. I was oblivious this time around that I was going to miss his protective presence.

The innocence of my youthful gaze inhaled the majesty of the countryside. As a child blessed with bucket loads of imagination, dragons were easily spotted emerging from the craggy rocks and pixies peeked around every tree. I had entered a magical portal, a familiar gateway to all who have tasted the delicious land of the deep South West.

However on this occasion the sparkling wonder of Kernow would carry a dark shadow. A sinister murky chapter was waiting around the next bend. A nightmare was stirring. Chaos was waiting our arrival. It had reared its malignant head and was breathing decay and torment into the crevices of empty halls and vacant dormitories.

We were guests on an annual pilgrimage, where for a fortnight we had the honour and pleasure to stand in for the resident boys choir during the summer holidays. Our job was to grace Truro's magnificent cathedral with harmony, gusto and vocal glory. For weeks we had been rehearsing, stretching and waxing our voice boxes to reach the heights and splendour that would befit the task at hand.

We were afforded the time to drag our cases into the entrance hall and swig down a quick cup of tea before our stern taskmaster

Mr. Bellows loomed before us. To his great delight he herded us into the draughty practice hall for a quick rehearsal. He was determined that our visit would be remembered, that we would leave our mark on Truro. If he had known then how it would all have played out, that he would indeed get his wish, we would surely have shoved our things back up on the bus and headed hell for leather home.

Although my mind was meant to be focused on singing, it had strayed, wandering off to the adventure of exploration. I pictured smugglers caves, peering in rock pools, slurping on clotted cream ice cream and jumping frothy white waves crashing in from the Celtic Sea.

"No, no, no," boomed Mr. Bellows. He was a towering man of fossilized features, his thinning hair swept across his head, with a thick strand of gray draped across his brow. Small rectangular spectacles perched on a huge bulbous nose. It was his nose that was the most striking feature, not only large and round, but pitted, and it shone, a glowing boozy red beacon. Smugglers of old would have given a right arm for that nose, the perfect answer to a moving lighthouse!

By his own assertion, he was strictly a ginger beer man, and those who harboured thoughts that he was a secret tippler, would never have dared voice them. Mr. Bellows was a daunting man, whose name reflected his presence. He was quick to temper, with a stern countenance. He could paralyze a boy in fear, like a giant bug hovering over its prey, preparing to suck the life out of its victim. His wrathful gaze shot terror through your heart, yet this summer I was to lose any feelings of trepidation and view him as a sad, lonely, and feeble old man.

"Concentrate boys, you sound horrendous!" He roared as spittle sprayed across those unfortunate enough to be in the front row. "Tomorrow night we are expected to fill the air with harmonic sounds that captivate the ear, not crucify it. Now from the top."

Practicing 'Turn Back O Man' for the ninth time wasn't exactly soul inspiring.

St. Peter's choir was an all male troupe from the small market town of Bury St. Edmunds. With the exception of a small gray haired man from Milton Keynes, the men were all permanent members of the choir. The gentleman in question was a fifty-year-old alto singer, who had recently suffered a breakdown, and had joined us in Truro as part of his convalescence. The boys also had an extra member to swell the ranks, Bobby White an angelic-looking bleached blond-haired boy with a dazzling smile and a cheerful disposition.

Truro's residential boys choir were on annual leave, offering us the opportunity to enjoy all the live-in facilities and the extensive gardens. The grounds were magnificent. There was an immaculate green square reserved for cricket matches only; it was made quite clear that this area was out of bounds, as was the small wooden pavilion set in front of the dark overgrown wood. Along side the main complex was a double squash court, a games room, and numerous sheds containing possessions of the residential boys choir. One of the sheds doors had a peephole, revealing several bicycles and a grand piano locked within.

Inside the building, we were permitted in our dorm, the games room at certain times during the evening, the practice room for rehearsals, and the dining room, which smelt of school dinners, mashed potato and pink custard.

The heavy oak doors to the kitchens were bolted until a large bell, suspended from the high rafters in the entrance hall, resounded signifying the next meal. The bell rope was for the use of staff members only. Try telling that to a group of mischievous misfits, hell-bent on destruction. I admit I was seeking adventure, but nothing could have prepared me for the sordid, violent, unpleasant chapter that was about to unfold.

The intense tone was set from the very first night of our two-week stay. Daniel Bright, a lean curly-haired teen, with uneven teeth, a cruel twisted grin, and divots in his face, from picking his zits, emerged as the unlikely leader of the pack.

James Fulton was Head Boy, a well respected red ribbon youth, with a cookie cutter boy next-door face, and an impeccable record. His reign as figurehead of the choir was about to meet a sticky end.

The militant force of Bright swept Fulton aside. His ruthless dictatorship slammed through our ranks like a stormy Cornish tidal wave surging over and swallowing sandcastles. The older boys and wannabe youngsters flocked to his dark banner. As a horde of hungry locusts sack a cornfield, they fed off his sinister convictions, all too willing to be men-at-arms in his army of terror.

Fulton's reputation was forever tarnished that summer. He became a trusted henchman, Tony Woods reluctantly followed suit, while Johnny Andrews reveled in the mayhem. Johnny quickly established himself as second-in-command, playing a mean bow to Bright's caustic fiddle.

We were sent to settle in to the boys' dormitory, a huge sparsely decorated room containing a score of iron-framed beds on wheels. Each bedstead was furnished with a wooden nightstand; the room also boasted a couple of porcelain sinks along one wall. Underneath a huge bay window several large chests were piled high. These presumably contained clothes and personal items belonging to the boys who lived here during the year. The adults in our party were all unpacking in adjacent rooms out of earshot of our abode

There were basic shower and toilet facilities down the corridor, clean but gloomy. The dormitory smelt musty. There was a wild scramble for beds. I found myself next to Bobby White the new boy, and Geoffrey 'Beaky' Harris, who had an oversize nose that hooked at its tip resembling a bird of prey. Hence the nickname that he'd been saddled with long before I first met him.

I was well prepared for the usual pranks that young boys played on each other. The previous years favourite was squirting toothpaste into a victim's hair as they slept. There was also the nightly moving of beds. Being as they were all on wheels, it was effortless to push a snoring occupant out into the corridor. Then there were the endless pillow fights, an accepted ritual, and part and parcel of our stay here the year before. Then there had been no Daniel Bright, and then there had been no daunting rules.

The door crashed open, Bright strolled in purposefully, closely followed by Andrews and Fulton. One of the youngest members of our troupe, Nicholas Pearson, had taken the first bed, just inside the doorway. It was a grievous mistake. Bright seized Pearson's suitcase and hurled it across the dorm. Unfortunately for Pearson the case was open, his contents flew everywhere. It immediately grabbed our attention. Some of the boys snickered as Nicholas whimpered, chasing after his scattered belongings. All laughter rapidly ceased as Bright screamed "Silence!"

He carefully placed his bag on the vacated bed "Now let's get a few things straight." he snarled.

"If you value your pathetic little lives you'll obey my rules. One, anyone leaving the dorm will only do so after asking my permission. In my absence Andrews, Fulton, and Woods will have the say. Two, if anyone dares to go into the woods at night, I will personally slit their throat." A knife sprung from Bright's pocket and was plunged into his bedside table. All eyes were focused on the silver shining blade. Bright released a chilling sadistic cackle that floated hauntingly cutting into the icy silence that his antics had created.

"Three, if I tell you to do something, you jump to it. Four, don't get cocky, don't piss me off and don't break my rules. The minimum punishment is a toweling."

"Get the fuck here," he suddenly screeched at Pearson. "Know what a toweling is?" he spat at the petrified boy.

"No" quivered Pearson, his eyes on stalks. Bright removed a long beach towel from his pack, slowly tied a hefty knot in one end, and wet the knot in the nearby sink. His face twisted grotesquely in a demonic snarl as he whirled the towel around his head and thumped it into Pearson's legs. One second Pearson was standing full of fear, the next he was knocked off his feet. As he curled up in a tight ball, Bright lashed the towel raining blow upon blow on the youngster's tiny frame. Pearson lay whimpering in a crumpled heap on the floor.

Open mouths gaped into the silence broken only by Pearson's tears. Fearful eyes flitted across the darkness of the dorm. "I'm not fucking joking. Do you understand?" We all continued to stare in bewilderment. "I said do you understand? You fucking half-wits." Grunts of affirmation, nodding heads, and shaky whispers brought a devilish smile to Bright's face.

"Okay, see you behave then. Right we're off for a smoke, anyone who dares to join us can leave the dorm." Dave Bull and Martin Chadwick, both eleven, but looking older than their years, joined the fourteen year old Bright and his appointed cronies. No one spoke; we all receded into our confused minds to explore the crazy demands of this new, uncivilized world.

Daytime brought relief. The ornately carved pews in the cathedral were our refuge. So were the beach trips, as long as Bright and his underlings could be avoided.

Away from the madness the lazy afternoons were bliss. There was solitude to be found rolling down the sand dunes of Perranporth beach. They also offered excellent hiding spots. I was looking through the long tall grass at the figures of Bright and his posse heading back up the beach toward the bus.

I had spent most of the afternoon with Bobby White the new boy. He had qualified for the holiday on the grounds that he'd sang for a number of years with different choirs in the Suffolk area. He probably wished he hadn't, Bright had already smacked his blonde head for no other reason than he didn't like pretty boys. Scott had the face of a cherub, large round electric blue eyes that were now gazing at the bus in sadness. It was time to return to the dorm, but before we got there, we had to face the bus ride and the dreaded torture seat.

Bright and company commandeered the back seat. Over the fortnight, all the boys, one by one, would be invited to join them. Whoever went would receive a going over, roughed up until tears stained dirty cheeks, all covered up by the laughing mob. If any of the adults saw anything, they turned away with thoughts of, 'harmless pranks, fun and games, all part of growing up.' It had amazed me that Bobby and all the other appointed victims, had traipsed so willingly to meet their fate, but no one had yet to defy Bright, until my name was called.

We'd been on the road barely five minutes when his leading henchman Andrews sidled up to me and hissed "Get your arse to the back of the bus Steed, we've got something for you."

"You might as well get it over with." Bobby urged. "It's not that bad." His claim sounded hollow, I had seen the tears in his eyes the day he was summoned.

"I'm not going." My voice was meant to sound confident, assured, but instead it dribbled onto the air as a thin, barely audible, whisper. The calls kept coming.

"Winky, get yourself back here."

The nickname stung my ears and ripped at my heart. I loathed being known as Winky, a name that I'd been endowed with by none other than Bright himself. As an adult I have pondered on the British way of labeling all of our body parts by their correct name, hand, ear, nose, shin, toe etc. yet we squirm at the anatomy of both men and women's sexual organs. To say the word penis is taboo for a lot of people, it is a 'dirty' word. So a host of names from 'willy' to 'knob' are used instead. My dad, as well as a lot of my peers, used the word 'winkle'.

Bright had made a huge joke that I had called my penis a 'winky', consequently the name Winky was thrown at me and unfortunately it stuck fast.

"You'd better go." Urged Bobby. His voice seemed distant. As if I was watching his mouth move in slow motion as though I was there and yet not there. I was gripping the seat so hard, my fingernails were threatening to rip through the padding. I was in turmoil.

The Clash would write lyrics several years later that succinctly described my predicament; 'If I go there will be trouble, if I stay it will be double."

I think in hindsight that my decision was made more from the fear of being roughed up right there and then for there was nowhere to run and nowhere to hide. Bright and his cronies would have their piece of flesh one way or another. For now though I would deny the vultures their prey.

"I'm not coming." I spat in defiance.

"Winky I'm waiting," crooned Bright in a singsong voice that was far gentler than its underlying intention. A voice screamed in my head "Please God, make them go away," and as the calls for my presence subsided, my stomach clenched in a sickly knot. Bright's rule number two thumped over and over in my head 'When I say do something, jump to it.' I'd broken the bloody rule, and time was running out.

The bus turned into the long driveway and came to a stop outside the halls of Residence. I was careful to stay in the presence of the adults during dinner, and when Bright organized a table tennis competition after we'd eaten, I felt a false sense of security in heading up to the dorm.

I was sitting on my bed writing postcards when the doors to the dorm were leisurely pushed open. Andrews strolled in with a beaming smile, followed by the wickedness of Bright. Pearson and Geoffrey Harris who had accompanied me upstairs scuttled from the room, dodging the staring eyes of the gruesome twosome. Geoffrey wasn't fast enough to avoid a sharp cuff across his head as Bright bellowed "Beaky" in his ear.

I sat rigid, fixed to the spot, like a trapped fly to the weaving dance of a spider. Andrews pulled two large towels from a radiator and passed one to the waiting Bright. They each tied tight knots in one end and ran them under the dormitory tap. Their movements were slow, deliberate. They meandered comfortably toward my transfixed frame.

"You know I'd pay a fiver to someone man enough to let me punch them on their jaw. One smack in the face for a fiver, are you man enough Winky?" I could feel the tears welling up inside of me. I mustn't cry I desperately told myself. Fear galloped through my body, seizing me in all its glory, I was suffocating in terror. Then from deep within something stirred, I heard my voice; it was clear and strong, with a sense of purpose.

"Don't you dare hit me," I roared. My words smacked the air with authority. The command caught Andrews off guard and I saw him falter. A rush of hope flooded through me.

"I fucking dare to hit you, you sniveling runt." Bright barked. His body language was clear; he was in for the kill. In a flash the onslaught began. I threw my arms over my head and tried to burrow into my sleeping bag. The knots came quick and fast raining in upon my body. I caught the full force in my stomach that stifled any screams. A sudden shot whipped through my guard and crashed into my chin. The pillow that my head lay upon was quickly dampening from my flowing tears, and blood oozed from my bottom lip trickling slowly down my throat.

The pounding towels whipped through the air in a heavy onslaught. I was scrunched into a tight ball yet somehow with all my force I screamed out. A primordial cry of desperation echoed through the dorm and as quick as the attack had begun, it ceased.

I had tried so desperately to suppress my sobs, to not let them see me cry. It was all to no avail as the tears ran freely.

"Hey Winky? Stop blubbering, we were only playing." It was Andrew's voice. "Come on Winky, you'll live." His voice was tense.

"Here let me see," cried Bright as he ripped my arms away from my head. He looked into my blotchy tear-stained face, my bottom lip slightly swollen and bloody. "It's just a bloody scratch, you're not badly wounded Winky. Man up. Next time do as you're told." Growled Bright as he flogged me one last time.

"Come on let's scarper." He sniggered as I lay sobbing into my pillow, as much in frustration and annoyance as in pain. The 'bloody scratch' duly healed, but I didn't know where to find a band-aid for a cut that could not be seen.

It was night-time that I feared the most. Left guessing who would be the victim, and what punishment would be inflicted. Bright's blade reappeared often, thrust into the nightstand as a reminder of his powerful command, and it wasn't just us boys who suffered.

On the second night of our stay, the gentleman on convalescence felt the full fury of Bright's sadistic rage. From dusk 'til dawn, raiding parties disturbed his sleep and abused his mind. Bright named him 'Earthworm', and with support from Andrews, he quickly incited all of the choirboys, myself included, into conducting lightning attacks. The name Earthworm echoed down the corridors. Loud howls and creepy caterwauls rebounded around the walls. Having the only bedroom on the first floor, supposedly for extra privacy, had left this fragile old man totally at the mercy of our evil plot. He tried to confront us, but Bright stood before him and screamed Earthworm into his cowering face. He jumped back into his room like a startled rabbit. At first light he was packed and off: he didn't even stop for breakfast.

An apologetic Mr. Bellows returned alone from the railway station with a face as black as thunder.

Oh he chastised us all right, using his full height and rolling his eyes to great effect, but he was doomed to fail. Bright ruled supreme with both an ironclad fist and a forked tongue.

Night-time commonly thought of as fright time, reached its climax toward the end of the second week. Bright had seized a pack of playing cards off Chadwick. Each card portrayed a naked woman in a fancy pose. Bright announced that it was game night; we were all summoned to take part. A card was dealt to each individual and the person who was judged to have picked the 'ugliest woman', had to strip off, and run around the dorm presenting his wares to the eagle-eyed audience. The rush of relief was incredible when a boy picked what was deemed a 'stunner,' but we were all playing a loser's game. Bright was the judge and jury, and eventually all of our bodies were paraded to the night.

At last it was lights out. Mr. Bellows had peeked his head in, totally oblivious to the sordid details that took place behind his back, he was obviously in a rush or he would have surely questioned why Pearson was standing stark naked in front of all the boys.

"Chop, chop, time for bed, lights out." He hollered sweeping out of the dorm, totally satisfied that we would obey his every whim. I closed my eyes, rushing to meet the world of dreams, even if it meant a tooth pasting, anything to hasten the dawn chorus and seek refuge on the pending day trip.

I craved the sanctuary inherent in the countryside of Cornwall. To be away from Bright's glare. Amongst the sand dunes, the cliffs and the sparkling waters that constantly kiss the land I could return to the colourful dance, the unspoiled magic of childhood. A world where faerie is real, and Merlin's cave echoed of dragons wings, mysterious spells, and hoards of sparkling treasure. Bright had certainly tarnished my world, but he would not destroy it. This night however, dreams were cancelled. Instead nightmares were on the menu!

Bright's 'game night' had only just begun. I, like several of the boys, had snuggled into my sleeping bag, pretending to be in the land of nod, but each and every one of us quickly resurfaced as towels were knotted and the threatening voice of Bright pierced our ears

"We are playing Dare. Anyone feigning sleep will be toweled; it will be the worse fucking toweling of your miserable life. Well take a look at that, Andrews. I've awoken the fucking dead." His chilling laughter harmonized with Andrews' acidic snorts, seeing all of the sleepers springing up like puppets on a string. I wonder now what went through the other lads' heads, as we unwittingly danced to Bright's manipulative song.

Boys having to masturbate, run to the dorm tap and try to stick their penis up it, assume sexual positions with noises to match. I counted myself lucky only having to show five positions of a man and women humping. I had no idea what to do. Being totally oblivious at that tender age to the fascinating world of women, my poses were rather unusual to say the least. I am sure they had as much to do with sex as Bright did for human rights! Still when the majority of your viewing public is in the same boat, they were easily entertained.

It was Tony Woods who suffered the humiliation of Bright's most twisted dare. Tony was always hanging back when the towelings were being given. He was the most reluctant of Bright's servants. A mild mannered youth, whose temperament did not live up to his nickname of Wolfman. His physical features left you in no doubt of who was being called when the yells and howls of a Werewolf filled the air. His dark complexion, long drawn face, with thick black eyebrows running the length of his brow made him the butt of endless jokes. His eyebrows met in the middle, giving the appearance of having only one eyebrow instead of two, and he was tall for his age, so he slouched to compensate, which gave him hunched shoulders and an awkward gait.

All torches were directed at his miserable silhouette. Bright's instructions were vividly clear.

"Stick you finger up your arse Wolfman and scrape a piece of shit onto your fingernail." Tony Woods scowled, someone snickered, probably Andrews, others groaned. I was grateful that this was Woods' dare and not mine. He certainly had my full sympathy.

With a look of utter contempt, Wolfman withdrew his finger, but no faeces could be seen. "Stick it up further, it shouldn't be too hard, you're full of shit," gloated Bright. I wasn't sure if Wolfman was pretending, because his fourth attempt revealed no sign of crap either.

"One more chance and then you're in for a fucking beating," hissed Bright. Woods' face was taut, his jaw clenched.

This time the tip of his finger was, according to the scathing howls of Bright, smudged with a speck of brown.

"Fulton, smell his finger." Bright ordered.

"I don't need too. I can see it from here," squeaked a ruffled Fulton.

"I said fucking smell it. You're a brown noser. You kowtow to Bellows; now be a brown noser in front of me." Fulton shuffled slowly across to Woods' bed and incredulously followed Brights' command.

"Well done," mocked Bright. Fulton hung his head low as he retraced his steps to his sleeping bag, and Woods looked relieved that the whole ordeal was over.

"Now lick your finger Wolfman, you fucking beast."

Woods' jaw wasn't the only one to drop to the floor. He looked hard at his shit stained finger, and then pleadingly at Bright.

"Lick it!"

All eyes shot from Bright to Woods. For an instance Tony Woods looked as though he was about to erupt, own his nickname and rip out the throat of his persecutor, but it was just a fleeting glint of disobedience. A desperate notion that quickly dwindled, and with it, died all our hopes for justice. There was to be no mutiny. Tony Woods slipped the finger slowly between his lips, and darkness shone brilliantly through the silent screams of midnight.

The bell that signified breakfast was served sang out loud and clear. It was strictly to be used by staff only. The major drawback to this was the bell rope hung within easy reach of little hands as well as big. There wasn't a night that went by that it didn't chime.

The bells rang out long and hard, night and day. It amused us greatly. The surrounding neighbours were no longer seeing the funny side of our monotonous prank.

In the dead of night sound travels, and Mr. Bellows' hairy ear was being blasted by several sleepy townsfolk who were showering him with complaints. His ranting and ravings were becoming all too familiar. On the penultimate day he gave us all a dressing down, he talked of honour and pride, he made threats to tell our parents about the flaming bell. If he thought we were listening he was way off the mark. He was full of bluster. Too many despicable nights of Bright's laws had tainted any thoughts of honour. A ringing bell seemed a mild offense to what had already taken place. A minor crime compared to the hell of the next 24 hours.

There was a feeling of trepidation; the atmosphere in the Halls was strained. Mr. Bellows took it that his talk had hit home, but it was Bright who was to strike destructive and deadly. I watched in amazement as he roused the demons in Andrews, Bull, & Chadwick with Fulton and Woods tagging along.

They smashed the windows of the cricket pavilion, and then embarked on digging up the carefully prepared cricket pitch. Their ungodly prank drew the attention of several of the boys who witnessed the carnage, but somehow Bright always managed to carry out his destructive assaults behind the backs of the adults.

Mr. Bellows went ballistic. We were all marched unceremoniously to the practice hall. His face was boozy red and he was set to burst. He ranted, he raved. He waved his arms wildly and gave his most menacing glare over his wire-framed glasses, a look that a week ago would have brought a boy crumbling to his knees. He demanded names. Those of us that had information had been warned off. A steaming choirmaster was nothing to the threat of the psychotic Bright. I buttoned my lip and cursed myself for being weak.

Mr. Bellows was stonewalled. Our mouths were buttoned; no one was prepared to cross the wrath of Bright. In his intense furor, Bellows threatened to drag us all home in silence and shame, he raged about the damage, he chastised us for the bell; he condemned us for the treatment of 'Earthworm'. I bet now that he wished he had loaded us up on the bus right there and then and driven non-stop for Suffolk. Maybe it was the thought of the final concert, his commitment to have us sing to the end, or the belief that his severe rebuking had finally found its mark. Whatever his thought process, regrettably we stayed.

Immediately after Mr. Bellow's curses, I found the courage to make a change. I voiced an idea to Bobby, a strategy that would be perceived as outright rebellion. We had discussed it before, but had never dared to implement it.

There was an adjoining dormitory that was locked; it was strictly out of bounds. If we had the key, we could gain a night of solitude, a welcome respite from the chaos we'd known. Bobby and I were talking openly, excited to dream of our heroic quest. We had left all the other boys in the dining hall and climbed the stairs to the bathroom. It was the ideal place, away from prying ears, to fathom out how to execute our plan. I was washing my hands; Bobby was drying his, when we heard a toilet flush. In horror we watched as the stall door was pushed slowly open. Time stood still as we waited for the occupant to emerge. Tony 'Wolfman' Woods strolled out.

Our panic stricken faces were mollified with Tony's soothing words "Count me in, I'm on your side. Do you think any of the other boys will join us?" His unexpected response was music to our ears. None of us were ready to openly betray Bright to Bellows; however we were more than willing to attempt to avoid Bright, to claim a safe haven away from him and his mob.

Geoffrey Harris and Pearson needed little persuasion, especially when they saw Tony was with us. Peter Sullivan was a different kettle of fish. He was a quiet unassuming lad of twelve. He had suffered the towelings and torments, but he saw our actions as openly defying Bright's rules. For a moment I thought he was going to expose us, but Woods' threat of retribution stilled his tongue. Although he wouldn't join us, he agreed to turn a blind eye. We considered his wavering a close enough shave, so we abandoned our recruitment strategy and went in search of Mr. Bellows.

Our request was simple enough our reasoning was coated with half-truths. We explained that it was fatigue, the other boys kept us up at night, we were asking for the opportunity of a full night's sleep. Mr. Bellows tried one more time to get us to incriminate someone, but to no avail. Seeming satisfied that we knew nothing, he granted our wish, and told us to collect the key after evening cocoa.

The final concert went exceedingly well. It seemed to put a bounce back in Mr. Bellows' step. He kept faith with the men's choir and joined their nightly ritual of frequenting the local pub. As soon as dinner was over they abandoned us for an evening of revelry. Thirteen boys left alone with only the pleasure of Mrs. Tee Hee's company.

Mrs. Tee Hee was Mr. Bellows' sister. If he was the gray storm cloud, she was the sun's shining rays. Her nickname reflected her extraordinary laugh. Most of the older boys poked continual fun at her, but I liked her. She was compassionate, a little ditzy and quite the talker once you got her going. I considered confiding in her about our night-time activities, but both Bobby and I didn't see how this gentle, fragile granny could stand up to the might of Bright.

Our excitement of plotting had been deflated when we realized the men had left without Mr. Bellows giving us the key. We sipped our bedtime drinks in silence, bracing ourselves for more of Bright's games. Mrs. Tee Hee carried two plates heaped with chocolate cake into the dining room. As boys greedily grabbed a chunk and wolfed it down, Mrs. Tee Hee whispered into my ear. "I have the key, why don't you round up the other boys and I'll unlock the door for you." The cake looked good, but the thought of freedom seized my attention. So while the ravenous horde devoured cake and sloshed cocoa, the five defectors smoothly carried out 'Operation Removal'.

We hastily gathered our belongings, thanked Mrs. Tee Hee for allowing us to keep the key, and locked ourselves into our newfound haven. I chose a bed and started to arrange my sleeping bag when Tony Woods chirped "Give us a hand, come on quick."

There was an edge of concern to his voice. "You don't think a mere locked door will keep Bright out do you? We need a barricade, look lively." We worked efficiently as a team. All of the unused beds were stripped of their mattresses and shoved against both entrances to the dorm, four wardrobes and several bed frames were dragged across the floor and rammed into place. We stepped back confident that our makeshift blockade would repel the most ardent of intruders; it was about to be put to the test.

Battle commenced as soon as our whereabouts was discovered. Bright was furious, and when we refused to admit him, the violence erupted. We could hear the splintering of wood, two wardrobes were kicked apart to make battering rams, two beds were smashed repeatedly into the walls until their frames bent and fell into pieces. Mattresses and pillows were ripped into shreds. It was a fierce vicious assault, first from one front, then from two.

With his force divided, they continued their onslaught of the main barrier, but a detachment, led by Andrews, was sent to storm the back door. Footsteps echoed on the iron staircase that led up to the fire exit toward the unmanned door. Tony rapidly split our group in two, Bobby, Geoffrey and I valiantly pushed against the wardrobes and mattresses, but we were fighting a losing battle. A window smashed, glass splintering everywhere, the manic faces of the mob were slowly but surely entering our space. Our rebellion was crumbling; a sustained effort was needed. We dug our heels in and pushed for all we were worth, but both doors were off their hinges, and the pack tore down the final obstacles that stood in the way of their impending victory. The siege had lasted a little over forty-five minutes. We were dragged callously back to the main dorm.

The thought of our punishment was surprisingly worse than the reality. A mass toweling followed with insults and jibes. The beating left a bruise or two, and my stomach churned in defeat, but somewhere deep within my bones there was celebration. We might have lost the war, but we gave battle, and in doing so, gained a measure of self-respect.

The five 'traitors', as we were called, were ordered to clean up the mess. We threw the broken bedsteads, torn mattresses, and shattered wardrobes into a heap. Pearson swept the scattered feathers into a large pile. We lodged the fractured doors into their frames as best we could and crept silently to our beds.

Bright, Andrews, Fulton, Bull and Chadwick went for a smoke; there was no invitation for the disgraced Woods.

Laughter echoed through the dorm on their return, another prank was in the works, and sometime after the lights went out we found out what it was.

I was shaken abruptly from my dreams from incessant banging and screeching. As I shook the sleep from my eyes I saw the ghost-like face of Mr. Bellows peering into our dorm. A desperate scream rattled from his throat.

Apparently his bedroom door was locked, his haranguing made it evidently clear that he believed we had been in his room and locked it from the inside. He wanted answers; he looked as if he was ready to break. It may have been the wild manic glint in his eyes that prompted Andrews to resolve the problem.

He of course claimed total innocence to the deed. He proceeded outside, and with the help of a ladder, he scaled the wall and climbed through the open bedroom window. In a jiffy the door was unlocked and Mr. Bellows stood and watched us as we all settled back into our beds. Peace lasted for barely a minute. Mr. Bellows quickly discovered that his light bulbs were all missing. This time his babbling shrieks fell on deaf ears. No one was prepared to take credit for the theft, and no one was about to point the finger at the culprits. He thundered out of the room slamming the door, and then stumbled blindly in the darkness.

His curses were loud, and there were several bangs and crashes. "He's fucking flipped," Bright jested. "Here Winky, take him this before he damages himself. Don't you tell him where you got it or else." Bright tossed a light bulb into the air, caught it, then handed it to me.

"Go on, quick," he hissed. His demeanor seemed calm enough, but I thought I detected a trace of weakness in his voice. Was Bright concerned that he'd finally pushed things too far? The answers to that lay in the events of the morning, and I couldn't have been further from the truth.

Bodies were flitting about early, packing backpacks and stuffing suitcases in preparation for our long journey home. Breakfast was served, and we were told to meet in the reception hall in one hour prompt, to board the bus. The wreckage of the night before lay undiscovered in the spare dorm. The key was back in Mrs. Tee Hee's hands and she had put it away trusting that we'd left it clean and tidy.

Nobody would discover the remnants of our war until we were long gone. I felt relieved that I would be saying goodbye to our summer abode; I swore that it was my last visit to the Halls of Residence. Next year I was giving this vacation the widest berth possible.

I climbed the staircase to the dorm to do one final check. A bursting sound of jubilant cries echoed from within. Inside a flurry of activity greeted my eyes. Bright's knack for rousing a crowd and creating mayhem, never ceased to amaze me. The large double windows had been pushed open, not to air out the room, but to conduct a farewell ceremony. On Bright's directive, Andrew's, Fulton, and a host of younger boys, including Pearson, were tossing things out of the window. A closer inspection revealed the contents of trunks, bags, and boxes, belonging to the resident boys choir, being hurled out of the window onto the pavement below. Clothes torn to shreds, breakables shattered, books ripped up and battered, and this was just the start.

Other lads joined the frenzy and I found myself charging down a flight of stairs, caught up in the energy of the moment. It was a release, an escape from the oppressed world of Bright's domain, but in our bid for self-fulfillment, we were once again exposed as puppets, merely pawns in Bright's power game. Shed doors were kicked open, bicycle tyres punctured, the front forks bent, a piano top was thrown open and the keys forcibly broken into pieces, a can of spray paint was used to splatter graffiti all over the shed, colourful swirls extended down the pathway, over the flower bed, finally exhausting the can with a frenetic dance upon the walls of the squash court. The surge of destruction had us firmly in its grasp. We aggressively ransacked everything in our path until our bodies hung limp, physically and mentally drained from our pernicious ire.

Mr. Bellows was on the warpath. He yelled until his face darkened in purple blotches, his eyes bulged and spittle dribbled down his chin. His manic screams fell on deaf ears. His scathing verbal attack washed right over me, I was too numb to pick up the shame that he tried to heap upon us. I had checked out. I desired to be home, away from the crazy reality of this mixed-up world, back to the comfort of my family and friends, who believed that we were being held in the safety of the church's arms.

The journey home was a blur, yet I remember our arrival. A stream of parents waving as the bus pulled alongside the church. I ran into the secure arms of my mother, watching other kids seeking comfort in the warm embraces of their loved ones. I looked over one last time at Bobby White; he had been my closest friend on our fateful trek through Cornwall. I knew he had absolutely no desire to step across the threshold of St. Peter's and join our choir. I felt a tinge of sadness as I saw his angelic face looking blankly out of a car window as he pulled away and out of my life. We had failed to swap phone numbers and it was with regret that I realized I would not see my friend again.

I reluctantly found myself at choir rehearsal the next Friday night. Mr. Bellows who always looked old seemed ancient; the years had tied themselves onto his features and woven themselves deeply into his heart. He looked broken. He gave it his best shot at pulling his body into an intimidating stance; he peered over his spectacles and tried desperately to put a bite into his bark. His glory days of putting the fear of God into a boy had slipped by with the waning tide forever laying submerged with the wreckage left behind us in Cornwall.

The aftermath of which was spelled out to us boys. We were told of the hundreds of pounds worth of damage that had been caused, our good relations with the people of Truro shattered, and that our church had been disgraced. Our yearly jaunts to Cornwall were cancelled and our choir remained firmly on home soil. It was then neatly swept under the carpet, a taboo subject. Our parents remained in blissful ignorance of the whole affair. The unspoken atrocities were to be erased from our minds by shutting our mouths and going about our business as though nothing had happened. I had a hard time shaking it off, yet I held my silence. I took the isolated trail of suppressing my feelings dealing with them alone, from within. My immediate response was to shut them away in a box marked guilty, ashamed and bewildered.

Bright's dictatorship faltered now that we slept in our own beds. He still caused havoc during choral recitals and rehearsals. Throwing his urine over the church heater caused a foul-smelling reek to waft down the aisle. We suffered the stench for the duration of a Friday night practice, but his actions finally caught up with him when, with Andrews, they stole the church collection box. He was unusually careless, and the Chaplain observed his theft.

Their dismissal from the choir brought me little comfort; I had lost faith with the church. I bowed out of the choir to pursue other interests. It was many years before I crossed the threshold of St. Peter's again.

EXCAVATING OUR STORIES

As I have worked on healing the pieces of this story I have pondered over several questions. I could never fathom why the adults never intervened down in Cornwall. Didn't they know what was going on? I know we didn't tell them, but why didn't they see it of their own accord? Why wasn't the supervision more comprehensive? Why was the devastation hushed up? Why were parents never informed of any of the incidents that occurred?

I still do not have all the answers. I knew that the first step for me was to leave St. Peter's behind me. The taste of Truro was stuck in my mouth and the aroma seemed so much stronger in a cassock and a ruff.

What I didn't realize as a boy was that when I walked away, the whole sordid trip would follow me. It would play out in my life and the lives of all of us who went through the torrid experience.

This is a truth for all of us, wherever we go our story goes with us. We are the pieces of our own living experiences. The importance is to own our stories, learn from them, embrace the pieces that serve us, and to release the pieces that hold us hostage making sure that we do not get stuck, trapped and lost in the story.

My Truro experience reared its head a couple of years later and bit deeply into my adolescence. A sight that I fully expected to warm my heart did the exact opposite. Moving from Middle School to Upper School seemed daunting until I saw a familiar face sitting at the desk opposite me. There before me was the beaming grin of Bobby White. I remember my excitement as he turned his face to look at me. For a moment the glint of recognition in his eye was for a friend who had been sorely missed. Then those large angelic eyes glazed over and hardened it was as though a steel shutter had slammed hard breaking the energetic connection from our hearts.

Instead of feeling the warm embrace of a friend, I suffered scorn and rejection. He announced in a booming voice so the to whole class could hear "Look who we have here. It's 'Stringy Bean.'" To this day I don't know why Bobby changed the name that he knew I detested of 'Winky' to a new name that I would grow to loathe with equal despair; that of 'Stringy Bean.'

At the time I could not fathom why a 'friend' would cut down an ally so harshly. As an undersized skinny youth with gangling limbs his mocking words stung. They also caught on like wild fire. The name stuck and followed me for three years through my life at upper school. The greatest hurt was that Bobby instigated it.

It took several years and many lifetimes within this lifetime for me to understand that I had copped the blast of his deep shame and anger, his own unprocessed baggage from our time in Cornwall. Seeing me was a stark reminder of his torment in Truro. It's strange how we deal with the monsters in our lives.

As the years drifted by, I looked to reclaim the story. It took fifteen years to share the summer of '74 with my parents and a few more years before I put the story down on paper. I thought about writing it with an element of the tall tale, where Bright gets his comeuppance, but this one cried to be written in all its gory detail. To see it in the fullness of what had happened as my memory recalled it. By doing so I found the actual events no longer held any power over me. I have been able to journey into the lessons and find the hero within.

I look at how carrying a name like 'Winky' and 'Stringy Bean' led me to kick out and strike as Bobby did, in a destructive way. My first job at 16 was washing dishes up at the local hospital. I devised a whole barrage of names that were hurled at my co-workers. I coated it with the tag of mischievousness and fun, yet the truth is it was downright mean. To go around shouting "coddy, coddy, coddy" at someone I had decided had a head that resembled a fish, a cod to be precise, was vindictive. To label a woman 'Pam the Man' and the list went on... All of these names were part of my own suffering, my own inner torment.

It was many years later that I discovered the power inherent in a name. I have already shared my own name Andrew Steed means 'The Strong High Spirited Horseman.' Andrew also has the meaning 'Manly' and Steed 'One Who Tends Horses'. I am always amazed at how many people are unaware of the meaning of their name. I asked this question of you in Chapter 1. Have you researched the meaning yet? It is a strong piece of medicine and one that I advocate that people look into. It is also wise to look up all the alternative meanings. You may find that one tradition has a stronger connection to your heart, for example; Mary means 'Bitter,' 'Star of the Sea,' 'Rebellion,' and 'Wished for Child'. Names carry a vibration that flows through us. It is therefore imperative that we work with the names that carry us. If a name does not feel right then we have choices. Taking responsibility we have the power to be the instruments of change.

Many women change their name on getting married. Some then divorce and keep the name they inherited in the marriage. I have met many women who no longer resonate with the name that they have taken. Many of them have continued to amble through life with a sense of displacement, an energetic unbalance that in their heart they know stems from the outlived purposefulness of their name. It takes courage to make shifts in our lives. Not everyone will understand. As well as potential resistance from family and friends the person will face a huge amount of administration work with changes to passport, bank accounts, utility bills and social media. Ultimately by doing the work we have the power. By embracing the name that feels right we open ourselves to the magic and meaning of that name to flow through us.

I have witnessed women who have reclaimed their birth name, their mother's birth name or a name that had woven itself into the fabric of their being with liberating results. I have also enjoyed hearing of people discovering the meaning of their name, the animal totems that are part of their family crests and for some the mottos that go with them.

Some women choose to keep their own birth name even in marriage. My daughter has claimed that she would like children one day, does not see herself getting married and if she does, will keep the name of Steed for herself and the children. Time will tell how this one unfolds. I do know that it takes incredible courage and a really strong woman and also a strong man to be open to this pathway. Both will need to be comfortable in their own skins with a willingness to allow each other to be fully themselves for this to happen.

The biggest lesson for me is taking responsibility and for consciously choosing the names I walk with. I have expanded upon this and work with journal questions in regards to our names in the next chapter. For now I leave us with my truth that any name given to us only becomes a part of us if we ourselves choose to own it.

What clinched it for me to dig through the Truro story and continue to reweave the strands was the recollection of seeing Geoffrey 'Beaky' Harris in 1991. I bumped into him at a party, oddly enough in the Rectory of St. Peter's. The Rector's son had become a friend of mine; his father had replaced the aging Rector of 'my day' with the choir.

Geoffrey was in a band with the Rector's son. They ended up playing a bunch of covers and a couple of originals at the party. As the evening wore on I had the opportunity to speak privately with Geoffrey. I mentioned the vacation in Truro. I asked him what he thought about the atrocities that we faced. He jutted out his chin, clenched his jaw, and denied that any of it had ever taken place. I could have cried for him. He hadn't just buried the chapter he had locked it in a casket and thrown away the key.

If we fail to claim responsibility as the author and hero of our own story we can easily fall into the role of victim. Peer pressure coerced an upright citizen like the 'Head Boy' Fulton who was swept away ferociously against his own nature. Without Bright's and Andrew's influence, Fulton would have made very different choices. His weakness and fear coerced him into a role that was very much out of character. Falling into a role where everything happens to us, where we get caught up being bent to someone else's twisted game can lead us to becoming numb, where shame shuts our mouths and hardens our hearts.

As for Bright, I am sure he was acting out the abuse that he suffered somewhere in his own life. As I have wandered upon planet earth/planet water I have come to understand that the only reason that any of us put someone else down is because in that moment we do not like ourselves very much. We strike out to hurt someone else because we are hurting. By diminishing someone else we look to put ourselves above the other person so that we can feel better about our own life, more important, more worthy. It is our own lack of self worth that drives this incessant wheel of judgement, fear and abuse. The challenge we all face is to become more cognizant of the roles we play. When am I an incessant judge? When do I become a collaborator to the judge's story? When do I refuse to become embroiled in all the gossip? When do I fall into the role of victim? Many people have martyred themselves and become stuck in their own life story. In my book 'The First Santa' I take a look at the character of Ebenezer Scrooge. A man who is vilified by most, a man whose name conjures up words like 'Miser, mean, grumpy, callous, tight-fisted, a kill joy,' generally an uncaring soul who puts a damper on the 'season of goodwill'. When I state that Scrooge to me is generous and a great gift giver I am often faced with perplexed expressions. When pressed someone will normally agree that he is big-hearted at the end of the story. I then ask, "Which part of the story are you stuck in?" "The beginning" is the response, which I believe accurately portrays the truth for so many of us on the planet. We have tethered ourselves to challenging stories from our childhood.

I wonder how many of the boys that were part of the summer of '74 still carry packages of shame stuffed into their bodies, wrapped in denial, tied up in pain.

I ponder how living on planet earth/planet water is so challenging for us all. Each of us has faced stories of abuse and betrayal. It is time to gently pull the strings that bind them to see the gifts. In the depth of despair lie the greatest treasures if we are only willing to look at them for what they are, opportunities to grow, to transform. We can release what no longer serves, reweave and look at the whole story from a different perspective. Our ending can become the beginning. Just as Dickens left Scrooge as one of the greatest gift givers, so we can dance in the light of our own presence. We can celebrate the fullness of the old adage; 'Yesterday is 'his'tory, tomorrow a mystery and today is a gift, that is why we call it the present!" So unwrap your gifts carefully and cherish them.

This story stands as a stark reminder to us all, to connect with our past, to forgive others and ourselves, and to let go. I pray that Geoffrey, Bobby, and all of the boys of St. Peter's find the riches from that summer.

I heard several years ago that Bright was killed in a motorbike accident. Nicholas Pearson the youth who received the first toweling down in Truro in '74 delighted in sharing the gory details. I remember that he jibed, "It serves him right; he got what he deserved." I take no delight in Bright's death. Would I ask to repeat that summer again? No, I would not wish that on anyone. However it happened. Bright came into my life for a reason and I am thankful for the opportunity to work through forgiveness to find a storehouse of treasures.

The Persian poet and Sufi Mystic Rumi summed up my feelings with these eloquent words;

> 'This being human is a guest house,
> every morning a new arrival.
> A joy, a depression, a meanness,
> some momentary awareness comes
> as an unexpected visitor,
> welcome and entertain them all!

Even if they're a crowd of sorrows
who violently sweep your house
empty of its furniture,
still, treat each guest honorably,
he may be cleansing you out
for some new delight.
The dark thoughts, the shame, the malice,
meet them all at the door laughing,
and invite them in.

Be grateful for whoever comes,
because each guest has been sent
as a guide from beyond.'
Translation by Coleman Barks.

Bless you Daniel Bright, for in your own twisted way, you pushed me along my pathway of self-discovery. I drifted away from the doctrine of the church, and found a deep faith in Spirit. I have developed a relationship with all that is, the Universe, whatever name one chooses to give to the connecting power of the Divine. To me this is simply abundant love. Love is within me and around me and can be accessed when I am present firstly with myself so that I can be present with others. A love that has invited me to look at the wonderful world of perspective that life continually offers. A love to weave and shine light into those harsh places where once darkness prevailed. In so doing I am finding fullness in my voice and freedom within my soul.

THE NEXT STEP; JOURNEY WORK AND/OR JOURNALING INTO A STORY

JOURNAL QUESTIONS

1. Reflect on one of the first times that you remember venturing away from the family nest, journal your experience and feelings. What did you learn about yourself? What were the challenges? What were the gifts?

2. Where has being afraid of the bully kept you from standing in your power? Where have you stood up to the bully? Where do you feel bullied right now? How can you shift the fear and find freedom from bullying? I used name-calling as a reaction to the hurt of having names I did not like thrown at me. Where have you struck out at others because of the hurts you were carrying inside? Where have you gone along with something that you did not agree with to fit in with the group? Consider writing 2 poems that mirror each other. One poem based on being trapped by bullying and one where you are liberated and free from bullying.

3. Where am I or have I been keeping quiet about something that happened to me knowing others are brushing the events under the carpet too?

4. Where are your safe havens, the sanctuaries in your life? Paint a picture in words or colours that describes the beauty of these places.

5. Where has a friend turned on you because they were hurting deep inside? Where have you turned on a friend because you were hurting? What do you need to do to forgive yourself and others to find more freedom in your life? It took me sometime to fully understand that forgiveness was never about the other person, it was always about me. For when I forgive I release carrying the burden of it all. If you are not clear about this spend some time journaling what forgiving someone would do for you. How would it make you feel if you were free from the animosity, anger, hurt that is wrapped up in not forgiving someone right now?

Bonus Question.
What question can you find to ask yourself from this chapter that has not yet been asked?

SHAMANIC JOURNEY WORK

1. Journey to look at the energetic disturbances caused by bullying in your own life, in the lives of other beings and in the land.

2. Journey to see where you have been playing the role of a puppet in your life. Working closely with a trusted guide journey to one of these times and cut the strings. With support of your guide and your witness self, help this part of you stand up tall. Dance and celebrate standing on your own two feet. Take time to integrate this work and then journey to explore other times you have or are dancing to someone else's strings.

3. Journey with trusted guides into the shadows and find a treasure chest that has been chained up. Inside this chest lies the unprocessed baggage, the perceived monsters in our lives. We are going to unwrap one layer only, open the chest, there may be other chests chained inside which we can come and open one by one later on. We are here not to slay the monster, we are here to befriend it. To find out why it hurts, why it hides, to not get stuck in the story and to help the beast step into the role of the welcome guest, to move from victim to hero. Please note this is an advanced journey so I strongly suggest working with an experienced shamanic teacher on this one.

4. Journey to an eagle or another bird that comes to help with this work. Ask them to take you to a nest where there are eaglets or fledglings and ask to merge with one of them to experience the feeling of leaving the nest. What do you need to fly into that requires leaving a safe haven to serve for the highest good?

5. Journey to make peace with the land. Go to a place where you desecrated or violated the land in someway and ask for forgiveness. Journey to a being who betrayed you in some way and offer forgiveness. What can you bring into the space within you once the gifts of forgiveness have been received and given?

Bonus Question.
What Journey can you offer yourself from exploring this chapter that has not already been suggested?

Chapter 6

Beyond the Horizon

We cannot discover new oceans
until we have the courage to lose sight of the shore.

Anonymous.

STEPPING OFF THE BEATEN PATH

My first taste of India is etched eternally in my mind. I had arrived
in what was then Bombay, during the middle of a sticky July
night, in 1987. The few Westerners, on the plane from Greece,
were all heading north, to Delhi, Rajasthan, and then up to
Katmandu in Nepal. Having never stepped out of Europe before
it would have been easy to follow the crowd. However, I was
listening to my heart. If they were all going north, I was traveling
south.

I decided on my arrival to follow a golden rule. I would wait
for the sunrise before heading out onto unknown streets, a wise
decision for a weary youth traveling alone. Waiting for the light of
the day to guide my way seemed to take an age. The airport was
packed. At least I thought it was. My perspective of 'crowded' was
about to change on heading into the swarming city.

As I looked around the airport lounge I realized I was the only
Caucasian face in a bustling crowd. My mind wandered to the
first time I experienced this. I was meeting up with some friends
and had sauntered into a nightclub in Brixton, London. My initial
reaction to being a minority of one was shock and trepidation
bordering on fear. I had proceeded with extreme caution, only to
be embraced with warmth and kindness. Now sitting amongst
a throng of Indian faces I was guarded; my senses were on
heightened alert. A group of men from Tamil Nadu befriended me

and I relaxed somewhat as the minutes slipped into hours and the darkness slid into light.

Looking through the story of my life I have had the experience many times in workshops, in the workplace, and even out and about on buses and trains of being the only man in a space. Rarely have I been amongst a sea of faces where I am the only Caucasian in sight. I found this to be a humbling experience, in a world where typically the white man 'acts' as if he owns it. It is powerful to shift things around.

Stepping out of the airport I was hit by an oppressive wall of heat. The torrid climate sapped whatever energy I had from my travel-weary frame. I remember looking at the bus that was the transportation to the city centre, and thinking 'how on earth did it pass its M.O.T.', its yearly inspection! As tired as I felt I was in no danger of drifting off to sleep; the helter-skelter bus ride kept me on my toes. I gripped the seat in front of me for dear life. The bus weaved in and out of traffic frenetically. Outside of the dirty bus window, the city was swarming with people; it reminded me of an ant colony that has been disturbed by a poking stick. People dashed in all directions, a chaotic weaving that had no beginning and no end. It seemed that every driver in Bombay had a death wish. Hooters constantly blaring, traffic dodging each other, narrowly missing pedestrians and other drivers by mere inches. One sign read 'Crossing the road can be a quick way to the morgue'.

The most difficult reality to swallow was the vastness of dilapidated buildings with widespread slums and excessive poverty. Bombay's city within a city was harsh on my eye and even harder on my heart. An abundance of huts made from straw, palm leaves, mud, corrugated iron, polythene bags and cardboard; I'd never seen such squalor. Watching poverty in third world countries on TV did not prepare me for the sharp shock of what my eyes were witnessing. My heart wept in jagged silence as the culture shock threatened to swamp me.

Taking to the streets was as crazy as negotiating the roads. The deluge of street urchins chasing after me for baksheesh, a handsome tip for finding a room, was suffocating. I was physically and mentally exhausted following the overnight flight from Athens. The stifling summer heat was rapidly draining my energy reserves. I was so grateful to crash at a moderately furnished Victorian hotel close to the Gateway of India.

India is a country of contrast. On reflection, I have memories etched in my mind of the utter devastation, poverty beyond words, a sadness that permeates and mourns somewhere in the depths of my soul. I also recall fondly, the humble, gentle people, the stunning architecture, the aroma of spices, the colourful processions, the majesty of a land as rich and diverse as my experiences were there. It is indeed a country of contrast. For me it was a journey of revelation, a true pilgrimage. I entered India very much a boy, and I would leave as a man.

One of the early revelations was that for the first time since my early childhood, I felt like I did not have to wear a mask. No one knew me. Nobody had any expectations of me. 1987 was pre-internet, pre-cell phone; I was beyond the reach of family and friends, as alone as I could possibly be in the world. A world that felt much bigger then. I was a small speck in a large land and it felt exhilarating. I was free to be, to fully explore me, emancipated from the constraints of society, I was liberated, uncontrolled and the wings of a free spirit lifted my bodies, mentally, physically and spiritually to new dimensions. Going to India helped me to remember and reclaim to walk and weave in this world in a very different way.

My stay in Bombay was brief. I knew immediately that I had to get out. I needed to find a less hectic setting; I craved space to orientate myself in this strange wonderful land. The confirmation came when I read the paper. The previous day there had been riots in Delhi, nineteen people had been killed, the story indicated that the trouble could easily spill onto the streets of Bombay, and I wanted no part of it. I bought myself a congress suit; a baggy lightweight white shirt and trousers, then feeling infinitely cooler I headed directly back to the airport.

I chose to fly to Goa. I remember being grateful that the main trading language in India is English. This made communication relatively stress free. I'm not sure how I got a ticket because the sales clerk vehemently told me that the flight was full, and then preceded to sell me a ticket. I was just relieved to leave the chaos of Bombay behind me.

I was even more grateful to get on the plane. A thin balding man kept repeating, "I'm so sorry sir, the plane is full". He then proceeded to usher me into the departure lounge and onto the waiting jet. I even had the luxury of a window seat. As we came in to land, acres of rice fields stretched as far as my eyes could see. Palm trees dotted the landscape. Goa was a gift of tranquility, exactly what I needed to acclimatize to this unusual, magical world.

I spent a week strolling along the surf and white sands that stretch as far as the eye can see, exploring temples, market places, steeping myself into the culture, and mixing with the colourful people of this unique region of India. Goa is heavily influenced by Portuguese architecture and religion. St. Francis Xavier's preserved body is in a coffin that hangs from the rafters of the Basilica of Bom Jesus in Old Goa. The tomb is lowered down for viewing every 10 years with the relics being kept open for worshippers to pay their respects and seek healing.

Having a mummified body in the house reminded me of what my brother had once said to my mum, "Do you want to be buried or cremated?" he inquired curiously. "I don't care. Just don't tell me", she squirmed, a shiver rushing down her spine. My brother thought profoundly, let out a rich belly laugh spluttering, "I think I'll have you stuffed and put on my mantelpiece!"

I arrived in monsoon season. Rain fell from the sky as if there were no tomorrow. Drenched to the skin one moment, and bone dry the next. As quickly as the rain soaked into my clothes, the bright hot sun that followed dried them. Waves pounded onto the shoreline, torrential rainstorms lifted the colours, the smells, and the tastes heightening my awareness of the vast beauty of this exotic land.

Though the Panjim streets were less packed than Bombay, public transport was still a trip! Bodies squeezed to bursting inside a rickety old bus, with stale sweat being somewhat masked by wafts of incense sticks constantly burned on every street corner.

Along with us paying passengers came the baggage from squawking chickens to baskets full of fruit balanced on heads. Sometimes we were desperately hanging onto the outside of the swerving vehicle as it surpassed capacity.

It was with a mixed sense of relief and glee that I jumped from the bus that pulled into Maria Hall in the sleepy fishing village of Benaulim. I took an isolated track through a timeless palm grove. I was rambling down a winding lane, carefree, singing Bob Marley's '3 Little Birds'. The bleached white sands of Benaulim beach stretched as far as my eyes could see. A deserted, secluded piece of paradise. Out of monsoon season Goa is packed with thronging parties and wasted wayfarers, now it slumbered, a serene welcome pace for this wide-eyed wanderer.

My tranquil demeanour was about to be shattered. A lithe, muscular youth, in his early twenties, was leaping across the rice field to my right. He swung a machete wildly in the air. I scanned the terrain; there was no one else in sight. I wanted to flee, but just like in a dream where you try to move and can't I was rooted to the spot. I gazed, horrified as he came ever closer.

His screeching howls lingered on the air. I couldn't make out what he was shouting, but it sounded ominous. Sweat was dripping even more profusely from my sun-drenched brow. The glint of the knife sparkling in his hand had the full attention of my eye. He hurdled a fence that was the only barrier between us. His feet gracefully landed six feet away from my transfixed frame. He tossed the machete into the air, caught it, and placed it between his pearly white teeth. Then with a mischievous wink he jumped at the bark of a coconut tree. No branches to hold on, he scampered up the trunk with the ease of a squirrel and the playfulness of a monkey. I realized my nails had been digging into the palm of my hands as I unclenched my fists. As quick as a flash he reached for the knife, swung it, and descended with a coconut in his hand.

Standing opposite me, he gave the widest grin, and held out both the machete and coconut. I shakily reached for the gift. My strength was completely drained; I tapped the hard shell feebly with the razor sharp knife. If the young man spoke English, I did not understand his version, I got his drift though, and handed the coconut and machete back to him. One clean slice, and swish, the coconut was deftly cut in half. He took one of the halves and eagerly tasted the fruits of his labour. He passed the other half to me indicating I should eat. I was so taken aback. What an amazing gesture. I beamed my thanks to him, grateful that I had been so wrong about his intent. Then I stared at the white flesh before me and I felt a shiver tickling up my spine. I despise the taste of coconut; it is the texture rather than the taste. It's the stringy consistency that I can't abide; it gets caught in my teeth and lodges in my throat. Interestingly, once cooked I love it! I pushed a piece of the dreaded fruit towards my quivering lips and started to chew. I tucked in and munched away tasting coconut in a way I never have before. I still to this day do not like eating raw coconut. Yet as I stood on that dusty track with a young man whose words I did not understand eating a fruit I couldn't stand my view of the world shifted. I looked into the sparkling eyes of my host and we both laughed. With thanks and bows I left this beautiful soul behind me yet his generosity is still with me today.

On my return from my explorations on the beach, I had a nap and then changed before heading out for dinner. I was staying in a small hotel in Panjim that boasted hot running water and electricity, not always the case in India. I also had the luxury of a double bed, curtains, dresser, bedside table, a fan, plus an ensuite bathroom, complete with shower, basin and a hole in the floor. This hole was my toilet, I was told it was a more hygienic way of getting rid of bodily waste; it was certainly a different experience squatting over a hole. I would soon learn that most toilets in India in 1987 were like this. I was careful to only eat with my right hand when out in public. The left one was for cleaning oneself after using the loo, a custom that I never embraced even though toilet roll was a rare and expensive commodity.

Before I decided to take the room I was careful to search for any infestations of rodents and roaches. Satisfied that it was clear and clean, I settled in to the comforts provided. I was in the bathroom when I urinated all over my trousers. That's not something I normally do; I certainly hadn't planned to do it this night. However it can be difficult keeping a steady direction when you are leaping around screaming "Ahhhhhhhhh!" I had never before had the experience of standing at a toilet whilst a foot long lizard leapt past my ear. In my hysteria, I had the good sense to dive out of the bathroom and slam the door. Once my heart rate had slowed considerably, I began to strategize. The song 'This Town Ain't Big Enough For the Both Of us', with the fixed stare of Ron Mael the Sparks' keyboard player flickered through my mind. One thing was for sure; 'Lizzie' had to go.

With a plan for action, I slowly opened the bathroom door and peeked in. My eyes searched ruthlessly for the lizard, I didn't want him dropping on my head. My right hand had a death grip upon my chunky hiking boot. If he wanted a fight, I was prepared. My chest thumped in anticipation, my breathing was quick, shallow. I searched every angle of the ceiling, floor and the walls, but to no avail. He must be behind the door. I swung skillfully into the bathroom and pounced. He wasn't there. My eyes took in the scene. I could see my anxious face in the mirror, my hiking boot still raised high, and the tap was slowly dripping water as a slight breeze flowed through the widow. That was it. The window was ajar; the lizard had made a mad dash for freedom. I breathed a huge sigh of release, dropped the boot, closed the window tightly, rested my hands on the sink, and looked myself fully in the eye.

Thank you, God. There was something extremely satisfying in knowing that I was alone again. I looked at my travel weary face. A brief smile flitted across it, which was quickly wiped clean as I accidentally nudged the mirror. Lizzie scampered out. I released an ear-piercing shriek, and flapped my arms wildly. It must have looked like a rerun. I dived out of the bathroom, whipping the door closed.

This meant war. I rooted for my other hiking boot; my right one was lying where I had dropped it on the bathroom floor. I composed myself, and then moved with purpose. It was quick and clean. I knew what I had to do. I moved swiftly, opened the window, and went on the offensive. I didn't want to hurt Lizzie, just evict him. Tapping my heavy boot behind his tail, I steered him towards the humid evening air. As he scampered out of sight I slammed the window shut. I then tapped the mirror vigorously to make sure there were no other lurking intruders and then congratulated myself. I looked into my eye and thought 'Andrew Steed, super hero, conqueror of the lizard!'

That night I drifted into dreamland with a sense of accomplishment. I'd outwitted a lizard. As daft as it sounds it seemed a big deal to me. I drifted serenely into the dreamtime only to be awoken with a start. The room was still, cast in darkness. It must have been the early hours, a deep silence hung in the air. As I lay in my bed it felt as if the whole room was moving. Something felt deadly wrong. I flicked on the bedside lamp and my stomach flipped.

The floor was chock-a-block full of cockroaches. Not your ordinary bug size roaches, these were nearly as long as my pinky and quite a bit fatter. My skin crawled, a sickly itching at the sight of those dirty creatures shuffling across my floor. I'm sad to say that in an instant, I lost it. I grabbed my boot and the crushing began. I was merciless. I went on a killing spree with a vengeance. A short sharp burst of fury, and the victory was mine. What of the war though? I knew there would be more. How had they got in my bedroom? I noticed a wide gap at the bottom of the bathroom door. Without hesitation I grabbed one of the blankets from my bed and stuffed it to seal their access route. I double checked the seals on my windows, and after some tossing and turning, finally fell asleep.

When the sunlight flickered across my face, and I had shaken off the last vestiges of dream world, I quickly surveyed the makeshift barricade to see if it had held. To my delight, all was well. My mind cast back to the image of those creeping roaches, I shuddered, something had to be done. I quickly dressed and I went on the rampage. I wanted to see the manager. As I stormed out of my bedroom door, a room boy, Madhu, witnessed my obvious distress.

"What is the matter Mr. Steed?" he inquired gently.

"I'll tell you what the matter is Madhu," I yelled. "Yesterday I found a lizard hiding in my bathroom, I chased it out, and then in the middle of the night I was visited by a horde of flaming cockroaches. I want to see your boss. I paid good money for this room, not to share it with the likes of a lizard and roaches!"

Madhu listened patiently to my ramblings without interruption. When I had finally run out of steam, he gazed at me quizzically, "You chase lizard from room?"

"Yes I chased the lizard from the room" I affirmed emphatically.

"Not good idea Mr. Steed" he sighed.

"What do you mean not good idea?" I snapped.

Without getting the slight bit flustered, and keeping a straight face, although I think there was a twinkling of laughter in his brown eyes he declared, "Well lizards eat cockroaches. If I were you Mr. Steed I would go pray for lizard to return. To have a lizard in your room is a rich blessing Mr. Steed."

Stunned, I slowly backed into my room. I felt incredibly foolish. My perceived foe was actually my friend. You can bet I prayed, but there was something far more important to do first. I needed to open the window. I could have prayed all day long, but with the window closed the lizard would have looked in on me and laughed, "He says he wants me, but he obviously doesn't need me." However I didn't get a lizard. I got two. The big one returned with a little friend. I named the longer one Lizzie and the other Lenny. They still made me jump out of my skin from time to time but I never saw another cockroach in that hotel again!

As for Madhu, he became a trusted friend during my short visit to Goa. Before leaving I invited him out for a meal to say thank you for his kindness. He was very thankful and he declined the meal. He told me one meal a day was sufficient and he'd already eaten. He was amazed at how much we eat in the Western world. I insisted on giving him something so he chose a train ride. He had never been on a train and it was a dream come true when I handed him a ticket to accompany me down the line with another ticket to return. Our journey took us past the Dudhsagar waterfalls. I'll never forget it for the look on Madhu's face and the sheer adrenaline rush that went through both of our bodies. We both hung out of the train door as we crossed the bridge by the falls. Beneath us was a sheer drop of over 100ft. It was crazy, exhilarating and absolutely awesome. It fueled the fire of freedom that pulsated through my veins. Where in the world can you hang out of a rattling train, moving at full speed, across a ravine? In 1987 in India, that's where!

EXCAVATING OUR STORIES

I included this tale without changing any aspects of the stories within this story. I chose to add these into this collection of reclaimed tales for several reasons. Firstly there are chapters in our lives that totally change us offering epiphanies or paradigm shifts. India provided this for me. It offered an opportunity beyond anything I could ever have dreamed of. I found a greater degree of both maturity and playfulness, a freedom of spirit that reached beyond my own horizon and the confidence and courage to follow my own winding trail in this world. I encourage us all to sift through the stories that we have weaved and reclaim the pivotal ones. In this way we can fully celebrate the greatness that has shaped us as well as reweaving stories that have previously clogged us up.

I giggle at the joy of receiving what I experienced with the coconut. In a country where there is so much poverty and imbalance, a man who had very little chose to offer his time with one of the fruits of his land without asking for anything in return. So often in this world people look to manipulate a situation. An offer is made with an expected return in mind. On this occasion two youngsters stood and laughed, our smiles lit up the sky and added to the radiant warmth of the sun. I pray that I may bring others as much joy as that man continues to bring me whenever I look at a coconut. I chose to use the word 'despise' in the story where once I would have written or spoken the word 'hate'. It is with gratitude that I have practically eradicated the harshness of that word in my life. I believe in some way that this man and this story played a vital role in that.

Within this treasured truth I reflect on the value of getting to know the whole story. Quick value judgments commonly leave a splattering of egg on my face. Being open and receptive to new ideas allows me to grow. Approaching life with my defence shields constantly up, blocks me from the rich rewards that an open heart full of unconditional love will bring.

What of the cockroaches? At the time that I lived this story I perceived them as an enemy, a most unwelcome visitor. I still would not be keen to share a living space with them. However, aren't they our brother and sister too? A hardy race for sure. A being that has adapted to life on planet earth/planet water and has been around far longer than us two-legged humans.

I have heard many people championing peace, unity and love who marvel at a caterpillar, whose oohs and ahs follow the flight of a butterfly only to voice disgust at a maggot and reach for a newspaper to swat a fly. I believe each being has a purpose and has as much right to be on the planet as I do. If we cry out that we need to save the bees and then kill a wasp because 'we have to draw the line somewhere' haven't we drastically missed the point? I hope this provides food for thought and a subject for discussion for us humans to partake in.

Lizzie the lizard also taught me a powerful lesson of opening the window for opportunity to flow in. How often have we requested something in our life and then not given it the access to reach us?

Another reason for including the tales of the lizards connects with name-calling. In around 1998 I was living in the USA. In my spare time I coached football or, as they call it, soccer. I was meeting up with a new team of players. A group of excited youth aged around 9 and 10 were gathered around me at the beginning of practice. Another coach whose team was sharing the same pitch came striding onto their half of the field.

The other coach was a woman who I recognized. Her daughter went to the same school as my children, I had seen her picking her daughter up from the school before. I had recently been into the children's school to share stories and the lizard tale had gone down particularly well. I always smile for it is a story that I have told both in a primary school and in a boardroom to great effect. It is how you share the tale that makes the difference.

As the woman went past me she called out "Hello Cockroach Man". My response was immediate I looked her dead in the eye and in a commanding voice I shot out, "What did you call me?"

"Cockroach Man" she stuttered as she saw my outraged face.

"Lady" I spat "My name is Andrew or Mr. Steed and if you can't remember one of those then simply Coach. I am not and never will be Cockroach Man. If you would like me to call you Cockroach Woman I will gladly oblige."

She stammered apologies and mentioned how much her daughter had enjoyed the story in school. I was glad her daughter had loved the story and that she had shared it on. However had I not owned my voice and rejected the nickname, the youth on the soccer team would have picked it up and I would have been known as Cockroach Man. Even if that had happened and the whispers behind the back spoke of Cockroach Man it would still be my choice of whether I took it on and owned it as my own. It takes courage to say NO; it also takes courage to KNOW that we are worthy to see ourselves by the names that bring us joy.

THE NEXT STEP; JOURNEY WORK AND/OR JOURNALING INTO A STORY

JOURNAL QUESTIONS

1. Where have I stepped off the beaten path in my life to go where my heart called rather than follow the crowd?
2. Look through the times in life when you have been in a situation where you were a minority of one. What were the challenges? What were the benefits? What have you gleaned from these experiences that serve you well in life? Has this helped you to be more open to others facing a similar situation? If so how has it helped you to be more open?
3. When have you been so wrong about what someone else intended? Where has a perceived foe turned out to be a good friend? Journal about a time when someone did the unexpected and your perspective shifted. Explore human friends and also look beyond humans for other examples too.
4. What is your epiphany or paradigm shift story? Look at the pivotal moments in your life story and then weave a reclaimed celebration tale.

5. Where do we want something to come into our lives and yet not give it access? Where do we need to figuratively speaking, open a window? As you explore this also take a look at how dependent you are on technology. What if you gave yourself a weekend being totally off the grid. If you choose to try this be sure to journal your insight from the experience.

Bonus Question.
What question can you find to ask yourself from this chapter that has not yet been asked?

SHAMANIC JOURNEY WORK

1. Journey to see if and where your defence shields have been raised to the point that they are blocking the flow of love in your life.
2. Journey to a cockroach and ask this ancient being 'what do I need to learn from you?' Once you have received guidance from the cockroach give thanks and journey on until you meet a lizard. Ask this transformer what windows of opportunity have I turned my back on and closed, that need to be opened in my life right now.
3. Journey to see where the flow of abundance is stuck in our lives. Where are we asking for something to come in without opening a window or doorway to allow it to enter?
4. Journey to ask our guides and ask which beings do I look down upon, feel superior to? What medicine do these beings carry and how can I learn to see them as my brother/sister?
5. Journey to ask what do I 'hate', detest, abhor? Where and how can I bring love into the harsh places in me so that I can bring love to the harsh places in the world?

Bonus Question.
What Journey can you offer yourself from exploring this chapter that has not already been suggested?

Chapter 7

The Unexpected Guest

The view was magnificent. I was staying in a beach hut on the golden white sands of India's stunning Kerela coastline. It was late August in 1987 and the South of India was fairly untouched from tourist eyes. Sitting on the doorstep of my shanty style abode I breathed in the beauty of this panoramic view, a slice of heaven on earth. The sun's rays glistened on the tranquil waves the rippling water gently caressing the fine grains of sparkling sand. Large leaves of coconut trees gracefully danced in the refreshing breeze.

I tantalized my taste buds with fresh mangoes & papaya, hand delivered by a young fruit seller. Every day twice a day without fail a frail slip of a girl who looked no more than 12 years old would stroll to my door, plant herself there and the only way to move her was to buy her goods. Even on the day that I refused to answer the door pretending I wasn't there she got me. I may have been close to 12 years her senior, but this spring chicken, was none other than a wily old fox.

She hammered on the door for a while and then plunked herself down on my doorstep all the time chatting away to me. She knew I was there and figured quite rightly that she could wait me out. The beach hut was fine to sleep in, but I didn't want to sit inside in that gloomy stifling dankness all day. Needless to say, when I surfaced, she left with her load a little lighter. I was astounded at how she carried such a heavy fruit basket on her head. Lifting the sheer weight was impressive enough, adding in the balancing and carrying act made it quite remarkable!

My arrival at Kovalam beach was quickly followed by her first visit. I hadn't even unloaded my pack from my back before her face was smiling sweetly at my door. Two mangoes and a bunch of bananas later I watched her glide off through the palm trees in search of her next catch.

The beach huts were simply furnished. A large room with mud walls was adorned with a well-worn mattress, a sturdy wooden bed frame, a chipped dresser and a night table. The thatched leaf roof hung over the walls leaving a large gap where the mercenary mosquitoes could fly, cockroaches could crawl and a friendly lizard could dart on in. I remember thinking all lizards are welcome. A door opened the way to the tiniest bathroom imaginable. No shower but there was cold running water in the small sink and the usual hole in the floor for a toilet. I flung the bathroom door closed and kept it that way until it was a necessity to open. I lit copious amounts of incense to mask the pungent odour that threatened to fly up my nostrils and catch in my throat every time I ventured inside. The rent was cheap, the room basic but what made it all worthwhile was the view, and oh, what a view!

I found a palm tree to lean my slender frame upon, and sat contemplating my good fortune. The spirit of the wind sang of freedom, it touched my heart, and I swear I could taste the timeless treasures and exotic riches of this unspoiled wonderland. It was my grumbling belly that told me that I needed more than a mango to satisfy my appetite.

It was late afternoon as I skipped along the sand to find a restaurant and any sign of life. The only buildings near my beach hut were four other small shacks and the occupants were all out enjoying the beauty of the day. The fruit seller had advised me to follow the shoreline for a while and then cut through a line of trees to where a small stream meandered down into the sea. The shade of the trees provided interesting shapes and shadows from the eclipsing sun. Before long I had located the stream. The water felt refreshingly cool splashing over my feet and ankles. In the distance I could hear the sound of a sitar and my stomach followed my ear.

I congratulated myself on my tracking skills for sure enough nestled in the splendour of a palm grove sat a rustic old restaurant. The decor was not much to look at but the food was divine. The good news was that everything was cooked from scratch the bad news was the time that you have to wait before tasting the delights being served.

The sun had long kissed the earth good night as I scooped the last morsel from my plate. I bought a bottle of fizzy pop, left a generous tip and headed off to my bed.

As I left the music and lights of the restaurant behind me I searched my day bag for my torch and realized that I had left it back in the room. I was going to have to retrace my steps in the dark. There were a few twinkling stars but it was a new moon night so darkness reigned supreme. No street lights to guide the way. As I stumbled through the tree line I could hear the sound of the ocean and knew all I needed was to find the small stream I'd crossed on my way to dinner, cut through the palm grove and the beach would lead me home.

A piece of me was glad I had forgotten my torch. Once my eyes had adjusted to the light I picked my way quite effortlessly to the stream. As I stepped into the water I was ready for the coolness that was about to greet my toes I just wasn't ready for it to shoot up my nose. Where I was expecting the firmness of land I found flowing water. My legs buckled as my feet met the sloppy muddy bottom and I found myself scrambling around in a deep pool of water. I lurched towards the safety of the bank, my over active imagination conjuring up snakes, rats and spine chilling creatures slithering in the dank murky depths.

I hauled myself out to safety noticing that one of my brand new leather sandals was missing from my right foot. I imagined it stuck fast in the gooey gunk less than five feet away from my grasp. It wasn't the first time that the waters had claimed my footwear, I was eight when my yellow flip-flop had floated off into the Mediterranean Sea on the island of Ibiza. I had naively thought that someone on a remote island would find it and think it was an exotic fish. I knew full well that no one would be chewing on this piece of leather, and I for one was not going back in after it!

I wish I had been as noble as Gandhi. I had read a story whereby Gandhi had hopped aboard a train one day and in so doing one of his sandals slipped off and landed on the track. The train was already moving so there was no chance of retrieving it.

Without hesitation Gandhi calmly took off his other sandal and launched it back along the track close to where the first one lay. When asked by a fellow passenger why he had thrown the second sandal, Gandhi smiled and shared "The person who finds the shoe lying on the track will now have a pair they can use."

I didn't feel noble and this generous gesture did not occur to me. I was busy hobbling up the sandy stretch sopping wet in search of dry clothes and the meagre comforts of my modest abode. I dried off quickly put my bottle of soda on the dresser extinguished the candlelight and snuggled into dreamland.

A loud crash ripped through the tranquility of my dreams. I shot up, ears alert, eyes quickly adjusting to the blackness of the room. The crash was real I just knew it was. Something or someone was out there or even worse they were in here! I fumbled for matches. I lit the candle on my bedside table. I scoured the room and breathed a huge sigh of relief I was alone. I slowly climbed out of bed and moved towards the door to double check the bolt.

Out of my peripheral vision I saw sharp shards of broken glass scattered on the floor at the foot of my bed. A dark pool of fizzing liquid stained the ground. It was the remnants of my soda. A half eaten papaya lay at the foot of my bed. My mind trickled towards the inevitable something was in my room. I spun around scanning the terrain as a hawk in search of prey. My eyes nearly sprung off their stalks as I zoomed in on the intruder.

A massive rat squatted menacingly in the corner of the room. I swear he was 18 inches long and that was without adding the scaly tail. What happened next was classic. I screamed, bounded onto the bed grabbed the covers for all they were worth and thrust them around me defensively protecting my throat.

Then we settled in for the western style stare out. We glared at each other, our full attention fixed eyeball to eyeball. 'Never corner a rat,' those words swirled through my mind. I was desperately trying to stay cool. I had no health insurance. Rats carry rabies. How long had the rat been in my room? A stream of endless thoughts raced around my head. He had obviously climbed up the dresser to knock the soda bottle down that meant he could have climbed up on the bed, climbed all over me. I wanted to close my eyes and pretend it was a bad dream but the rat's squinty little eyes were boring into my brain. I had to do something. A random thought flashed up yet again of the flaming Sparks singing 'This town ain't big enough for the both of us.' The lizard had turned out to be my friend but a rat?

No, no, no, one thing for sure was this room was not big enough and it was Ratty who would have to go. The problem was how to remove him. Nervously I started to ramble "Look rat I paid a fair price for this room and I rented it as a single. Did you hear that you furry ball of bubonic plague? I don't want to hurt you but you have got to go." I blurted it all out loud it was nervous talk, a way of trying to raise my spirit.

"I'm not leaving" he spat back. My jaw nearly hit the floor. I was flummoxed totally bewildered I could have sworn that the rat had just spoken. I was still trying to rationalize the moment when he did it again. "I'm staying put. I like it here. It's quiet except for you blabbering on. I'm claiming this as my new kingdom." Any fears that I was harbouring dissipated I was totally flabbergasted and this led to intrigue.

"I... I never heard a rat speak before." I interjected softly.

"What do you know, human?' He snarled in contempt. "I am not any old rat. I am the King of all Rats. You address me as your highness you long-legged lanky excuse for a human. Let my words penetrate your feeble little mind. Every King Rat has a voice and I will be listened to. If only I could find my useless subjects. They are always hiding, running away, why if I caught one of them now I'd give them all such a whipping with my tail, I'd bite them into shape, I'd... I'd..." His huge frame trembled in anger, his eyes glowed with the flame of destruction and then it was over his shoulders hunched and that big grumpy old rat began to cry, large salty tears dampened his fur and streams of tears trickled onto the earthen floor.

I was now thoroughly bemused. What do you say to a bawling rat? "King Rat" I awkwardly began. "Why all the tears? Is it because you can't find any of your.... Peop... rat...ty..subjects?" The sobbing intensified, a damp patch was rapidly growing around his bulking frame. "Have you ever wondered why other rats run from you?" My words fell on deaf ears.

"Oi Ratty" I hollered. Instantly the tears were extinguished as his heated glare sought out the insult. "King Rat" I continued coolly, "Have you ever wondered why your subjects hide from you?"

"You simpleton" he chastised, "I am their King. I am he who is to be obeyed; they are my servants. I don't ask stupid questions. I give orders. I instill fear, I am the strongest, most ferocious of all rats, I will have order in my kingdom."

"Is that so?" I mocked. "Look King Rat, if you have order, why are you skulking around in here. Take a good look around at this room, your new kingdom. What a lonely, dark, damp existence."

"No more lonely or dark than it is out there." He sighed. Again his body slumped as if the weight of the entire world was upon his back. As I looked at his demeanour I felt his sorrow. All thoughts of mocking him evaporated into the stillness of that moment. I spoke from my heart hoping my words would reach his.

"When I arrived here today your kingdom took my breath away. Out there amongst the dunes is a paradise. The sun sparkles on the ocean, fruits hang in abundance on the trees. I admit when the sun goes down a piece of me is afraid of the night. We humans have got so used to shutting ourselves up in boxes we separate ourselves from the natural world. It is fear, we fear the darkness and we fear the unknown. We have turned our back on the wild ways, we have forgotten to honour the cycle of the moon and the turning of the seasons. We look for security by building walls to protect us, which in time can easily become our prison. You crawl into this dark space and talk about making this dank dark hole your Kingdom, trading all that beauty for this small room? Well you're welcome to it go ahead stay put and live in fear." My words seemed to linger echoing in my mind as much as his.

"I'm scared to go back out there." I don't think he meant to reveal as much, this involuntary admission made him spit out

"I don't have to go out there, no-one can make me. I'm a powerful king!"

His terror was real you could almost smell it. I recognized that fear. It was one that I have danced with on many an occasion. I love adventure yet I fear it. I thrive on being around people, yet I also crave to be alone. I yearn on being loved and on loving with an open heart yet I pull and push away at times feeling so lonely, so alone, that it hurts. I have seen this fear in the eyes of so many lost souls, we humans drift along desperately seeking to love and be loved searching for a friend who we can fully trust. That was it. This search for love for friendship is what had brought us together.

"We long for friendship, we desire to love and be loved in return." I suddenly realized that I had voiced this insight for the giant rat was chewing over the word friend. It seemed to be jammed in his jaws, caught in his teeth.

"You need a 'ffffriend? You want love. Pathetic human. That's your weakness. I wander this world as a King. All should bow and cower before me. My title demands that love and respect is shown." He sneered derisively.

"Ratty" I bellowed. The sound of my voice echoed eerily, catching both of us by surprise. There was genuine concern on his face. I definitely had his full attention so I pressed home my advantage "I miss my friends back in England, I miss sharing your beautiful kingdom with the ones that I love. I also needed space from everyone, like you I ran away at some level. I needed to be a friend to myself so I can carry the beauty within me. This is a daunting task sometimes. I am weak not because I need a friend but because I fear the intimacy that friendship brings, I fear the power of light and love as I fear the very darkness in my soul. When I saw you in this room I looked at you with loathing, you were a filthy rodent to be exterminated but you are so much more than that, I am so much more than that; you are my reflection, my brother. What I fear and loathe in you is what is inside of me and as such both of our kingdoms are tainted with long shadows of darkness, but there is hope, I..."

I'd obviously gone far to deep for the king of the rats, he interjected with "I had a friend once, he annoyed me one day so

I ripped his throat out. If ever I go back out there I'll sink my sharpened teeth into those slovenly servants behinds."

"Well you've tried that approach and look where it's gotten you." I retorted. "Go ahead though, most of us humans do, we try the same thing the same way and expect it will be different this time, that's the definition of insanity Ratty!"

"Quiet human! It's time for my nap!" He had tuned me out. He sank his full weight into the floor and closed his eyes.

The realization that I was rooming with a rat, even if he was my 'brother' was creeping me out. I went to try and reason with him again, but the thought 'try the same thing the same way and expect a different result reverberated in my mind. I looked at the snoring rat, was he drooling? I had to do something. I edged gently off the bed still clutching the covers to my neck. Slowly but surely I silently shuffled my way to the door. The dead bolt slid back with relative ease. I unlatched the door to the looming darkness beyond. With the door wide open I crept soundlessly back to my bed. I reached out and grasped my left sandal the right one being entrenched in the mud somewhere in Ratty's forsaken kingdom. With all my might I hurled the redundant piece of footwear at the shack wall. I had no intention of hitting or hurting the rat, but I was ready and willing to claim my own space. The sandal whipped through the air and crashed into the wall inches from King Rat's chubby rear end. His response was automatic he leapt forward alongside the wall toward the door. I claimed the initiative, raining coins, from my bedside table, against the wall, as each one bounced back onto the floor the chunky rat darted towards safety. He scampered away from the assault hurtling to freedom through the doorway and onto the cool sand. As his tail slid across the threshold I bounded behind him and wedged the door closed. He was gone, "Yes please" I shouted.

It was some time before I entered the world of dreams. I sat on my bed listening to the sounds of the night, watching the shadows to see if he returned. When I was finally convinced that my sleep would not be disturbed I snuggled under the blankets to digest and integrate the rich rewards gleaned from this midnight visit.

EXCAVATING OUR STORIES

The story is based upon a treasured truth. Right up to the moment that I bounded onto the bed wrapped the covers around me and stared at the rat is how my memory recalls the events that night.

The following is a synopsis of what really happened. After what seemed like an eternity I edged off the bed, covers in tow. I moved cautiously to the door and slowly opened it. I then retraced my steps and sat hoping and praying for the rat to leave.

I knew a cornered rat feeling threatened will strike. I had no insurance and I was frightened. He was huge, I recall him being a bruiser of a rat, plump and at least a foot and a half long though that might have been the night-time talking.

When it became apparent that he wasn't going anywhere I grabbed a bunch of matches and pitched them one at a time behind him. My heart leapt with joy as my plan worked. Every time a match hit the wall the rat edged along it. Then at last he saw freedom and made a mad dash for it. I was in hot pursuit, I slammed the door closed, locked it and bolted back into bed.

Needless to say I kept no more fruit or food in the room and I prayed hard that no more rats would come a calling. I am grateful that the rest of my journey was, as far as I am aware, rat free!

One of the benefits of writing a reclaimed tale in the tall tale format allows one to explore a scenario from a creative perspective. The rat talking was initially a tall tale yet the rat did speak that night, I just didn't hear. In formulating this version I hear him in many ways that offer opportunities for introspection and growth.

THE NEXT STEP; JOURNEY WORK AND/OR JOURNALING INTO A STORY

JOURNAL QUESTIONS

1. I left fruit sitting out, a great temptation for a rat. Journal about a time where you left something lying around that brought unwanted attention that was at first uncomfortable or difficult to deal with. Examine what gift came with this challenge.

2. When was the last time you went out into nature in the dark? Take a night hike in silence and sit for a while listening to the song of the wild. I remember taking a group of inner city youth on a summer camping trip in the USA. We headed out down an unlit trail with no torches to a waterfall. We went in silence and remained that way for the whole experience. We sat listening to the cascading falls and were entranced as thousands of fireflies danced a symphony in front of our eyes. It was a magical moment. More so because of the looks of awe on the youngsters faces and their exclamations of wonder once we had returned to the campfire. After your experience journal what you noticed internally and externally.

3. Where do you find yourself doing the same thing the same way and complaining about the result? It is always good to be aware of a pattern that is keeping you stuck. Take a look at where you are like a hamster on the treadmill running and going nowhere. Once you have identified this pattern journal what life would look like if you changed it and went a different way.

4. Journal where you feel powerful in your life and where you feel less powerful. What could you do to breathe more power into the places where there is less power?

5. In the story I state 'I also needed space from everyone, like you I ran away at some level.' Where in your life are you creating space and healthy boundaries for yourself? Where do you feel your space is invaded? What are you running away from? If you were to stop running and face your fear how might things look differently than they do now?

Bonus Question.
What question can you find to ask yourself from this chapter that has not yet been asked?

SHAMANIC JOURNEY WORK

1. Journey to find a guide who will be the one you can go to help you face your fears. Ask them for insight on the root of your fear and where it is manifesting as drama in your life.
2. Journey to seek where in life are you giving away your power in relationships.
3. Journey to meet the part of you that is hiding in the corner and ask how can I be a better friend to you? Ask how do I love myself more in healthy ways?
4. Within the story the theme of being an outcast comes to the surface. Journey to ask where in your life do you feel like an outcast and how can you shift this energy to feel like you belong.
5. In this story I stepped into the water expecting it to be at the same level as it had been before. Journey to the water and ask where am I in the flow and where am I blocking it by assuming things will always be the same. Where do I do the same things the same way and expect a different result.

Bonus Question.
What Journey can you offer yourself from exploring this chapter that has not already been suggested?

These are some of my thoughts to work with this story. What are yours? Maybe you found another aspect of yourself within this tale. I invite you to delve into these and all stories. Have you reclaimed any of your own yet? Have the courage to explore the vast array of riches inside of you. The stories are your treasure map and you are the key.

Chapter 8

A Shamanic Initiation

This last story mirrors the first story with its Celtic connections. This one goes deeper as I explore an initiation into shamanism and earth medicine. I will give both the background story and also an insight into the characters that appear so that the story makes more sense to the reader.

Firstly here is a synopsis of what I experienced when I was 9 years old as a cub scout: I was in a troop that met in Hogs Lane in my hometown of Bury St. Edmunds. Akela is the title given to the Den Leader. The name is associated with wisdom and comes from Rudyard Kipling's Jungle Book. Akela is the Wolf and as such all the boys who join the scouting program become wolf cubs. For Halloween one year our leader, Mrs. Letzte, invited families to attend a party. I remember her fondly. She was a diminutive woman with a huge presence. She seemed ancient, a wrinkled face with sparkling eyes and an overbite. She laughed a lot and yet there was something otherworldly about her. Although her countenance was light and loving she had a stern glare that brought a boy into line as quick as a flash. I look back now and think she could easily have been from the world of faerie.

The Halloween party was going to be a highlight, we were all buzzing in anticipation. All the cubs were going to dress for the occasion where we would play games and tell stories.

I had gone home with the thoughts of being a Devil. When my dad agreed to make a wooden pitchfork and my mum said she would sort out the costuming I was in heaven. I couldn't wait for the big day to arrive. That was until I saw my outfit. To start with it was black. I did everything in my power to convince mum that the devil was red even sharing Manchester United football club as an example. They are known as the red devils and they play in red not black! There was no winning this one.

Worse was to come. The top half was okay; a black polo neck sweater was comfy. I wasn't sure about the horns that looked more like cat ears to me but nothing could have prepared me for what was to be adorned below the waist. Sheer panic gripped me in a vice and I struggled to find breath let alone words. My mum had gone shopping in the high street retail store Marks and Spencer where she had purchased a pair of girl's black knickers. She had sewn a long black tail onto them. I was an incredibly skinny kid and showing my legs off was barely comfortable in shorts. I would have felt undressed in underpants so you can imagine my chagrin slipping into knickers! I remember that I felt like I wanted the earth to open up and swallow me. I can still see the other boys' smirking faces. When Mrs. Letzte called me to move into the front row to stand next to her and another boy who was a 'red devil' I could have died. We both had pitchforks and I am sure my face matched his long red corduroy trousers. A night to forget, a memory to push away and never recall was how I initially viewed this one but perhaps not. I am excited to say that once reclaimed, it was and is a night to remember!

In my reclaimed story I will work with:

Akela - The Wolf Pack Leader.

The Cailleach - In the Celtic tales she is the old crone. She is also known as Beira, the Bone Mother and Cerridwen - she has connections with both the wolf and the sow.

Hell - In our western world we have associated Hell with the Devil and it has become a place of fire and brimstone. An older view is that Hel is a goddesss in a similar vein to the Cailleach. She is Queen of the Underworld in Norse mythology whose role was to look after the souls of the dead.

Blue Woad - A plant known as Isatis tinctoria, Glastum or Woad produces an indigo blue dye which is associated with the Picts and Celts who painted their bodies in it before going into battle.

Samhain – Modern day Halloween.

Sovereignty – The great goddess of the land. The Celtic perspective, and for that matter my own, is we either live in dominion over the land or in Sovereignty with it. Dominion over is where we see ourselves as being more important than other beings and that the land is there for us to cut up, own, sell, parcel up and do with as we please. Sovereignty with the land is about being in relationship with all beings, where all things are connected. I love this idea and wish I could tell you that I am always in this place. I am not. I move ever closer to being in Sovereignty. I look to honour the land and all beings and when I forget I gently remind myself to come into alignment and treat all with the greatest respect.

Morrighan – Goddess of battle/war. The great queen who is the harbinger of death associated with crows and ravens.

The Wild Hunt – Connected to ancient folklore and ritually re-enacted amongst Gallic and Germanic tribes is a collective shamanic journey that I work with every year at Samhain. It is one of the most profound rituals that I know where we stand up for life. We go into battle dressed in blue woad and sweep clean all negative forces that look to rob the worlds of prosperity. In the Irish epic the Second Battle of Mag Tuired the Tuatha De Dannan alongside the men of Ireland sweep clean the Fomorian gods of chaos. We symbolically recreate this whilst singing home the lost souls of the dead and helping the Bone Mother when the veil is at its thinnest.

Marks and Spencer – Looking up the meaning of the individual names for the store gives another twist to the story. Marks means the God of War and Spencer is to dispense or give.

Red, White & Black – The colours of life, death, and rebirth. Also the colours of night, day, and the betwixt and between, the sunrise and sunset.

To Hell & Back

The She Wolf, the Pack Leader, the wizened one raised her craggy throat and called the community to gather in the thinning veil of Samhain.

Mrs. Letzte, as she was known in her public persona, was ancient. Her face furrowed and etched from a lifetime of stories,

a road map of joy, sorrow, wonder and wisdom carved into her leathery flesh.

Some whispered that she could shape-shift, that her den, which was in Hogs Lane, was named so because she could be seen rooting in the earth, on a dark moon, half moon and full moon night. There were rumblings and murmurs that in the guise of an old sow she worked her magic there. She was tiny in stature and yet her presence was huge. When she laughed, she cackled. Her jaw protruded so that her bottom teeth un-naturally enclosed her top teeth and her eyes glinted with a knowing that went way beyond this mortal realm.

Word had it that she used those gnashers to ferret out and grind properties from the earth that she scattered into a giant cauldron for making potions and salves.

The general consensus amongst the boys in our troop was that a kiss from Mrs. Letzte would be your last, the kiss of death. Perhaps that was what brought the glint to her eye, for the wise ones know that there can be no life without death; that in the ever-spinning wheel the last will be first. The Old Sow, the She Wolf, the Last One, the Cailleach, the Crone, the Bone Mother, Beira is known by many names. And in the guise of a Cub Scout Leader the Hag prepared the brew.

She had invited the families to enter the lair. Us boys were told to dress for All Hallows Eve. We would gather in candlelight and listen to eerie tales around the hearth. A boy's imagination lit up with images of ghosts and ghouls, goblins, sprites and devilish imps. In my mind's eye I conjured up an image of the Devil with a trident for roasting sinners in the fire.

I shared the gory details with my Mum and was delighted when she said she would sort out the costume and my dad would carve out the devil's tuning fork. It was going to be a special night.

My elation crumbled into disbelief, dismay and utter despair as I slipped into the clothing picked out by my Mother. To begin with it was black. I argued that the Devil was red until I was blue in the face. Somewhere beyond my consciousness, deep in the veil, the Cailleach chuckled as she painted me on the wall in her cave. She mixed woad in a bowl of bones and smeared it on my cheeks. She was claiming me, preparing me, painting me in the battle colours of the clans and in that moment it was beyond my thoughts and way beyond my control.

Worse was to follow, as I looked at myself in the full-length mirror. My black horns that jutted from my head could so easily be mistaken for cat's ears. The black polo neck jumper hid the red blotches that were growing on my neck, yet my face gave me away as the heated glow of embarrassment coursed through my veins. I was wearing a pair of girl's plain black knickers with a drooping black tail sewn on to them. My gangling lily-white legs completed the scrawny ensemble. Somewhere beyond my consciousness, deep in the veil, the Cailleach chuckled as she stroked the black cat, the guardian animal at the gateway to the Underworld.

Knickers, girl's black knickers. The tag identified them from Marks and Spencer. I screamed inside, the fury of battle raged within me. I wanted to die, I felt defenseless, oblivious to the fact that in the veil the old ones laughed, for they knew that I had been marked and given to the Gods of War.

I remember thinking that I had been sent to Hell. And somewhere beyond my consciousness, deep in the veil, the Cailleach chuckled. Her withered clawed hand reached out for me in the ethers and pulled me close. Her foetid breath crawled across my skin and she kissed me. I died a thousand deaths. I was in Hell. Her cackles fueled the fire. The red roaring fires of Hell were calling and I was being groomed to rake out the glowing embers and dance upon them. I was stepping beyond the guardian black cats into the depth of the Underworld. The Great Goddess, in the purest form of Hel, had chosen me. The Bone Mother, Cerridwen, Biera waited.

Her mortal form beckoned me to step forward into the light as I sought the darkened corner at the gathering in Hogs Lane. She saw me; her piercing eyes gleaming in the light of the fire. Another boy dressed from head to foot in red with a trident at his side had a devilish grin from ear to ear as he looked at me squirming on the sidelines. A couple of boys had snickered at my discomfort. As I raised the large trident that my Dad had carved I grew in stature. My face was glowing red from the mortification of parading my pallid lanky legs before the Pack, but as I walked into the light my chin jutted forward and I radiated an air of defiance. This was a battle and I would not go down without a fight. She truly saw me. Where the boys had scoffed, she cackled, and it was a joyful sound to add courage to a battle cry rather than scorn upon it.

I stepped out cloaked in the colours of the raven's wing, with pasty ashen legs protruding awkwardly and a shining red face. Somewhere beyond my consciousness, deep in the veil, the Cailleach chuckled. She had called me to the cauldron, on the Samhain feast, dressed in the colours of life, death, and rebirth. Clothed in black, she saw the Morrighan's wing mark my shadow and her own bony fingers touched my heart. The trident was my pitchfork that unbeknownst to me would serve coals of love one day, my own relationship with fire would blossom beyond societal norms. Little did I know then that I would train in the ancient art of firewalking, a practice 1000's of years old, a transformation ritual that indigenous tribes all over the world embrace. I was destined to lead firewalks in the new world and the old.

It also represented being marked for the Wild Hunt for going into battle with the three prongs; 1. To stand up for life and sweep clear the Fomorian gods of chaos. 2. To help the Bone Mother in her season of Samhain as we pick up the bones of the dead and 3. To keen home the lost souls, those who have not yet crossed. I saw my Mum's beaming smile as I stepped to Mrs. Letzte's left and the seeds were sown for this boy to grow into a man. The Goddess held me close balancing feminine energies in a masculine body. I looked into Mrs. Letzte's twinkling eyes as the Mother watched the Maiden watch the Crone bringing me closer to Sovereignty, bringing me into her undergarments and holding me there, teaching me to make love to the land.

EXCAVATING OUR STORIES

As I found a voice to this story I realized what a pivotal moment this was in my life. I was 9 years old. Nine represents 3 times the 3 levels of being. There is magic in the number 9, when multiplied it always adds up to nine. As I pieced together the core elements of the tale I was astounded how it reflects my life's path and passion.

I know my mum will cringe when she reads the first part of this story. We have never talked about it. I had forgotten it. It was buried deep inside me. It actually came flooding in when I was listening to my partner Joyce share a related experience. When she was little Joyce's mum dressed her in a traditional eastern dress for a Halloween gathering. She had craved to be a princess and 'fit in' with the other girls in her school. She already felt like an outsider as her family had moved from Scotland to

Germany. A tall skinny girl who spoke a different language felt more ostracized than ever in the ornately hand-sewn dress. Just as I was ushered to the front, her teacher singled her out for special attention. A gesture of acknowledgement for the stunning dress caused her unwanted attention, embarrassment and pain. I am pleased to say she has reclaimed that story. The gift in her sharing was it brought my experience of being a cub scout bubbling to the surface.

My mother has wonderful healing qualities. Her mother was incredibly intuitive. They both are what I would call wise women or healers. The hereditary healing qualities have been passed down the female line from mother to daughter until there were no daughters to pass the lineage on to. I feel in my bones that my mother passed these attributes to me. I have no living sisters. The balance of the masculine and feminine is strong in me. I am named for both the masculine and feminine. Andrew being manly and strong and Steed is the totem animal that represents the goddess and the land. In essence my name means the Strong Manly Goddess!

I was mortified at the time pulling on the black knickers and now I see the story as such a gift. It is amazing how it all falls into place to reflect my choices in life. I strive to bring the masculine and feminine energies into balance in me and in the world. I work closely with the Morrighan and look to walk in this world in Battle Truth rather than War Rage.

Life on this planet can be harsh and challenging. Each day is a battle. When I stand in Battle Truth I honour someone else's perspective whilst honouring mine. When in War Rage I try to cut down someone else and force my view of the world into his or her face. Being a father and having a son brought this lesson to the forefront of my story. When my son became a teen he started to grow his own set of antlers. The problem was there was already a Stag living in the house. He started to stomp his feet and was ready to rut. Well there was only going to be one winner, room for just one King. We went at it hammer and tong. I was crushing his spirit whilst burning my own. Fortunately I woke up. This was my son and I love him beyond the horizon and back again. The last thing I thought I would ever do is end up harming him and yet there I was creating war with him in our own household. If I didn't make a change I would send him out into the world in the shadows of my own wrathful footsteps. It is interesting how many people will say, "I am against war," without being cognizant of all the wars they are fueling with their own words, thoughts and deeds. Families, communities, social media sites, religious organizations, political groups, sporting affiliates, whole countries, in fact all relationships are places where hatred, animosity, jealousy and mistrust can fester into war. The saying 'the pen is mightier than the sword' comes to mind. I use the sayings 'may we all learn when it is appropriate to sheath our tongues so we create less wars in our own back yards' and 'We have two ears, one mouth, we are able to listen to twice as much as we speak'.

I used the shamanic tools that I have learned and been gifted with to facilitate the change in my relationship with my son. I took my anger to the fire and released it. It was a powerful transformation. I have continued to live my life walking into my own shadow to shine the light there. To figure out who am I? To know myself intimately, to love myself unconditionally so that I can bring this light and this love and shine brightly in the world. Reclaiming stories is part of this profound journey. My relationship with my son has blossomed because of it!

Doing the work works! So much so that both my children and I chose and found a way to live together in an argument-free zone. My daughter was 17 and my son 19 years old respectively, the three of us shared a 2-bedroom flat or, as they say in the States, apartment. It was my last year in the USA, the kids had their own rooms and I slept in the front room. We had dinner together every night and shared stories about our day. The way we managed to live for that whole year and a day without an argument was we listened to each other. We did not always agree and we knew we would always be heard. It was quite an education. My daughter readily declares it is her favourite house that she has lived in to date.

In the reclaimed story I write; 'The trident was my pitchfork that unbeknownst to me would serve coals of love one day, my own relationship with fire would blossom beyond societal norms.'

I trained in 2005 to become a firewalk instructor. It was here that I transformed my rage into love. I forged a partnership with the fire. The tools of the trade are a pitchfork and rake. Both are used in tenderly working with the wood in order to prepare a bed of hot coals. As I stood clutching the three-pronged wooden trident I had little idea that I would witness 1,000s of people coming to the fire to dance through their fears into the manifestation of their dreams in the British Isles, Ireland, the USA and Canada. Please do not go out and light a fire and try to walk across it. You will end up in the intensive care unit with serious burns. However if you are called to understand firewalking look for a reputable practitioner in your area or email me and I will recommend someone.

The Wild Hunt is part of an ancestral calling. Gallic and Germanic tribes gathered to usher in the New Year. To help sweep clean the negative destructive forces and bring prosperity flowing to and in all beings. It is an experience that goes beyond words. If you are intrigued to learn more then I would suggest again you research a practitioner who facilitates this work. I recommend you check your teachers out carefully. As I always tell students, 'do not put me or for that matter any teacher up on a pedestal as we will all fall off. Teachers are people too. I am a man with a drum who is trying to figure it out just like everyone else.' The important aspect of doing this work is that you have to do the work; no one can do it for you. Any teacher worth their salt lives what they teach and does not serve their students any knowledge that has not first been marinated in their own life.

Through my studies I have worked with several teachers and I am grateful to Tom Cowan a wise elder in the Celtic Medicine tradition who I met many moons ago. It was under his tutelage that I learned the steps to integrate the work of the Wild Hunt into my life. Over the years of deepening my practice I have facilitated this ritual every year without fail sometimes twice a year as I have been called to work with displaced Celts in the USA and Barbados and with those who have often forgotten that we are an indigenous people here in the land of Alba. Tom gave me a framework, then Spirit through the guidance of the Morrighan and Biera, to name but a few, continually lead me to keep expanding the horizon of these teachings. I am currently building an outdoor medicine circle in Aberdeenshire to celebrate this work on the land in Scotland. I will also be weaving these ways in Canada in the foreseeable future.

In the Celtic story there are 3 strands of poetry that bring us to peace. These are sorrow, joy and peace. We only know joy because we know sorrow. Many people get stuck in the story and the pain of sorrow consumes them. This is fed often by fear and an unconscious anger. The work in keening home the lost souls in the Wild Hunt and being able to hold space for others to keen is a gift I will cherish to the grave. It is something that I look to share and pass on. I am grateful for it on so many levels. Never more than the day I walked into a High School and the teacher looked at me with a dazed expression and shared the turmoil inside of him and other students. Sitting on the floor with her head in her hands was a young teenager who I had not seen before. She was a best friend with a boy who was known to most of the students who were about to enter the classroom. The boy in question had returned home from school the previous night to find that his dad had killed his mother and then the dad had killed himself. The teacher was beside himself to know what to do. As I took in both his and the young girl's despair I knew exactly what to do.

I shared with the class how in the Western World we often hide our emotions. We learn to suppress them. Young men in particular are taught that it is not manly to cry. We shut down and block our feelings. There are so many people who walk around totally numb. Grief, anger, pain and fear are pushed way down inside.

I told them that to this day this practice is still honoured in parts of Ireland at a funeral or a wake. I explained that keening is lamenting, a wailing and crying that is laced with poetic verse that accompanies a death. This musical artistic expression celebrates both death and life. I demonstrated keening through a song that I was taught by a Medicine Man Yellow Wolf and the power of the song took them to a place where when prompted they opened their hearts and their voices and keened. As one youth gave permission to authentically release their cries onto the wind it gave permission for another to join in the lament. There was a ripple effect until all of the youth were in the full swing of the sorrowful song. As directed we moved our cries from sorrow to joy until we were all at peace. We wailed together in unison, for about 45 minutes we released the pain inside. Afterwards the youth were amazed at how much anger and grief had been wrapped inside of them. The overwhelming response was that they all felt so much lighter. Their courage that day will live in my heart forever.

THE NEXT STEP; JOURNEY WORK AND/OR JOURNALING INTO A STORY

JOURNAL QUESTIONS

1. We all have both a masculine and a feminine side. Many people deny one side or feel more comfortable expressing one side rather than the other. Take a look at both sides that reside in you and journal, which one is more dominant within you. Why is this? What do you love about each side? What do you fear about each side? If the whole idea of having both masculine and feminine inside of you makes you uncomfortable, journal on your discomfort.
2. Where am I creating war in my own household? Where does my war rage burn in other areas of my life? What one thing could I do today that would create less rage?
3. What gifts do I carry that I will cherish to my grave? What needs to die in me so something new can live?
4. Where do I stand in Battle Truth in my relationships with my family, friends, school/work, and community and with myself? How can I develop more authentic relationships with self and others?
5. The wise elder knows to howl at the moon like the wolf. I believe it is imperative that we let our wild self out in a safe and healthy way. When was the last time you howled? Going out in nature and keening, yelling out the sorrow, frustration and/or anger until you are laughing and singing is a healthy

practice. I look to take myself to a place where I am not near other people and then let my voice be heard. It is important that we shift the sorrow to joy and then to peace. Do not get stuck in the story!!!

Bonus Question.
What question can you find to ask yourself from this chapter that has not yet been asked?

SHAMANIC JOURNEY WORK

1. Go to visit the Land of Eternal Youth and find your child self under an apple tree. Under the visionary fruits of the underworld ask to be shown where you have faced shamanic initiations that have been forgotten in your story. Both falling into the cow dung and mud at Chadacre Farm and this story connect me to my shamanic pathway. What pieces do you have that are buried inside that once reclaimed will give more life essence to your journey?
2. Where is the balance of masculine and feminine out of alignment in my life? How can I address this? How does this misalignment affect the natural world?
3. Where do I harbour any animosity towards my own mother and/or father? How does this affect my relationship with the Mother and Father energies that I associate with the Earth and the Heavens?
4. Where does my war rage scorch the planet and any beings seen and unseen? Where is my battle truth supporting the planet and any beings seen and unseen?
5. Journey into the colours of life death rebirth into the strands of white, black and red to see how this never-ending cycle is part of your daily life and how it serves the greater picture of the Universe.

Bonus Question.
What Journey can you offer yourself from exploring this chapter that has not already been suggested?

If you have been through each and every chapter my hope is that you have ingested, digested and thoroughly enjoyed all that has been presented to you. My hope is that you have reclaimed stories from your own journey and that you are shining more brightly in the world. My hope is you will pick this book up often and continue walking into the shadows to take your light there. I wish you vibrant health, abundant wealth and heaps of happiness. Love...

Andrew Steed is a storyteller, Celtic shamanic practitioner, author and guide to sacred travel. He has been leading pilgrimages throughout the British Isles and Ireland since 1999. He takes people to love the land, to delve into the stories, to connect with the ancestors, the fae, the dragons and their own hearts.

He travels internationally leading Celtic shamanic retreats throughout the Isles, in the USA, Canada and the Caribbean. He is a Master Firewalk Instructor. He is an artist in residence for PA and a member of the Scottish Storytelling Centre.

He has pilgrimage routes that go to;

Scotland
o Iona, Mull and the Kilmartin Valley.
o Isle of Skye.
o Aberdeenshire.
o Isle of Harris & Lewis.
o Orkney.

England
o Northumbria.
o Cornwall, Glastonbury and Stonehenge.
o Glastonbury, Stonehenge and Oxfordshire.
o Cornwall and Devon.

Ireland
o Glendalough, Tara, Kildare, Newgrange.
o County Cork & Kerry, Skellig Isles, Burren.
o Gypsy Horse Drawn Wagon – Wicklow Mountains

Wales
o North Wales
o Anglesey.

There are plans for pilgrimages to the Isle of Man and to other nemetons in the Isles so please be in touch if you are called to wander in wild places with me. For those of you who are looking for an authentic travel experience that honours the wandering ways of the witness, rather than the mad dash rush of the tourist, I would warrant to suggest that you have found your guide.

Andrew also has a 3-year in depth study of Celtic Shamanism in the British Isles with enrollment open for 2015 and 2017 and beyond.

Year 1: The Swan's Cloak – The Path of the Bard
Year 2: The Sacred Outcast – The Path of the Wild Mystic
Year 3: Oak Knowledge – The Path of the Wise Elder

And a 2-year study in Bearspaw near Calgary in Canada beginning in 2015 with perhaps more offerings there in the future.

You can also study online through his innovative teachings on Celtic shamanism. Please email for full details.

He has 2 other books in print; 'Living at the Edge of the World in the Centre of Your Own Story' & 'The First Santa'.

For information on shamanic workshops, pilgrimages and storytelling email Andrew at asteed@andrewsteed.com, befriend him on Facebook and/or go to www.andrewsteed.com.

Julia Helen Jeffrey is a Scottish artist and illustrator. She studied painting at The Glasgow School of Art.

Her main artistic aim has always been to capture mood and feeling, as expressed through the human face and figure. Gradually, through the years, her work has come back closer to the things which first inspired her to want to draw and paint; the sense of magic in certain parts of the Scottish landscape, as experienced in childhood holidays, exploring ruined castles and clambering over cairns, and the incredible power of stories and legends to transport us to other worlds, and strengthen us in our own.

Her mythology and fantasy-themed work, of recent years, has attracted considerable acclaim and attention, with features in numerous fantasy art journals. October 2008 saw the publication of her first book cover (and illustrations) for the fantasy novel Lament (by Maggie Stiefvater), followed in 2009 by more sinister supernatural fare for fellow Scot Daniel McGachey's ghostly collection, They That Dwell In Dark Places. Her work also features alongside celebrated artists and best-selling authors including Neil Gaiman, Holly Black and Charles De Lint, in the illustrated short story collection, Ravens In The Library. The Tarot of the Hidden Realm, her first tarot deck, was published in the Autumn of 2013.

To contact Julia please go to www.stonemaiden-art.com.

Lightning Source UK Ltd.
Milton Keynes UK
UKOW03f0408100914

238301UK00001B/34/P